Spanked!

A
Black Velvet Seductions Anthology

In the Driving Seat © 2009 Richard Savage
Intimate Submission © 2009 Cara Bristol
Trusting Her © Copyright 2009 Starla Kaye
Secret Desires © Copyright 2010 Cara Bristol

All rights reserved. No part of this book may be used or reproduced in any manner whatsoever without written permission, except in the case of brief quotations embodied in critical articles or reviews.

All characters in this book are completely fictional. They exist only in the imagination of the author. Any similarity to any actual person or persons, living or dead, is completely coincidental.

Published 2010
Printed by Black Velvet Seductions Publishing Company in the United States of America

Visit us at:
www.blackvelvetseductions.com

Richard Savage

In the Driving Seat

Great to see you at the show

Ric x

www.blackvelvetseductions.com

In the Driving Seat

Barbara gritted her teeth, her father had been right, Alan was a pig! The indignity! How dare he do this! She loved shopping, but he always spoiled it by bitching about every cent she spent. God she hated this petty debate every time she spent a dime on herself. Couldn't he just enjoy the fact that she looked good?

His grim funeral director's face stared back at her over the breakfast table. Barbara tried to coax him out of his foul mood with what she hoped was one of her winning smiles. Alan sat there, seemingly unmoved by either her attempts to lighten the mood, or the aromas of coffee that mingled with the sweet pungent smell of grilled bacon, filling the kitchen.

He had the credit card bill open, lying accusingly in front of him on the table. His features looked as if they had been carved from a slab of granite. His eyes were cold and hard, as though he was about to announce some great natural catastrophe had occurred. This happened every damn time the credit card bill arrived and it made her feel sick to her stomach!

She found his rigid control over the finances unsettling, as if nothing in her life was really certain or stable. She had always found shopping a comfort, but Alan had destroyed the pleasure in that, making her feel guilty, with his constant scrutiny of bank statements.

She longed for the time in their early marriage when he had been lighter, before his constant nagging about money, when he had treated her like a princess to be pampered and spoiled. In an attempt to rekindle those early feelings, she tried to summon up a smile but saw not a glimmer of his mood melting.

A trickle of alarm slid through her, refusing to be squelched. He did seem more angry than usual this morning. There was something in his manner, coldness, and distance that hadn't been there before.

She watched as his eyes narrowed and his fork clattered to the plate. She shivered a little and moved in her seat as she felt a wave of cold wash over her.

Like a volcano, Alan erupted, "You have to be fucking kidding? This is a credit card statement?"

She watched as his cheeks flushed and his nostrils flared. She heard the rush of air over his teeth. He was barely containing his rage. His sudden ferocity shocked her. He had gotten angry before, but he had never exploded quite like this.

She felt lost, alone, empty in the face of Alan's explosive anger, and it frightened her.

"This is ours? Right?" He shook the piece of paper. "I was just wondering if I had opened the statement for the third world debt by mistake."

Barbara felt herself smile, involuntarily. She had always loved his sense of humor, but she hated it when he used it sarcastically. It was like having something she loved used against her as a weapon. Her teeth squeezed her lower lip, as she tried to suppress the deep sadness that filled her, threatening to overwhelm her. She'd felt herself succumbing to this familiar feeling of sadness and isolation as Alan had become stingier and stingier.

As she sat before him she felt her anger rising as she thought of him goading her. She found it frustrating, as there really was no reply to his sarcastic humor.

"Well? The shoes. Are they solid gold? Or what?"

"What the hell, do you know of style?"

"I know how fucking much it costs." She saw the muscles in his jaw go tight.

Alan felt the anger bubble inside him like the agitated fermenting of an angry sea. His anger was a boiling churning cauldron of bile, souring the taste in his mouth, as it frothed climbing ever higher on the inside of his mind. He saw red and boiled over. What the fuck was he to do with her?

His mind turned the events over, his patience at an end. It drove him crazy, that with Barbara it was all material things.

He knew her father had always given gifts to compensate for his lack of time with her. *Gifts—things instead of time.* He sighed. He could easily understand why Barbara equated gifts with love and why she believed that money could buy happiness but he hated that outlook.

The situation was desperate and as he sat there, despair clouding his thoughts his thoughts turned to the article he'd read in a magazine while waiting for a haircut.

The article had been about domestic discipline. The writer of the article had claimed that the introduction of spanking had saved his marriage.

He had read about spanking in adult magazines before and he found the whole idea arousing, but he had never considered it in terms of repairing his relationship with Barbara.

He rolled his shoulders. Maybe spanking would be the magic bullet that would save their marriage.

Her words from another fight over money came flooding back into his head, *"Maybe I could just ask daddy for my allowance back, or maybe he could give you a raise."*

He felt a moment of calm, that silent spell before the thunderclap. His fists came together in front of him scrunching the flimsy paper into a ball. "I hold the purse strings in this house! Is that clearly understood?"

"Yes Sir," her voice was small, that of a lost little girl, standing at the headmaster's desk.

She looked so innocent, her head cast down, her eyes looking up at him. There was the expression of a little girl sorry for doing wrong and it tugged at him making him want to wrap her up in his arms and tell her it would be okay, but he'd done that many times before. The other part of him was intensely irritated by her blatant attempt to manipulate him.

He knew this meek and mild stance was all a part of the game. She wanted to slip from the hook, as he had let her in the past. Yet he knew that he could not go on like this. This time he had to be strong, one way or another, this had to stop. A line had to be drawn.

"You have two choices. Either we go back to the shop and I stand there while you tell the manager that $1500 is a ridiculous price for a pair of shoes and your husband won't allow you to spend that kind of money or..."

Barbara smirked and half giggled at the absurdity of her trying to do that. The humiliation would be unbearable. She had shopped at that particular store since she had been old enough to buy her own shoes. The staff knew her. Returning the shoes like that was *not* an option

Alan's jaw tightened "You think this is funny?"

She watched as he folded his arms, a wall of defiant muscle before her.

"Your alternative is to submit to a spanking."

She felt her jaw slacken. She could not believe what she was hearing. He had to be kidding. She looked at him incredulously.

The wooden dining chair slid back on the kitchen's quarry tiled floor and he stood. She felt intimidated by his sheer physical presence as he drew himself to his full height, shoulders back, shirt tight across his chest.

Spanking? Surely he was not serious. Her stomach churned, this was crazy. She felt her hackles rising, as the thought of him spanking her filled her mind.

"This is a joke right? You *are* kidding?" She folded her arms indignantly across her chest.

He put his hands in his pockets, and rocked back on his heels. "I *am* going spank you," he said simply, in a matter of fact voice, as if he was announcing that it was time for supper.

He took a step toward her.

"You *are* the one that has to be kidding now! I have not been spanked since I was four."

She felt dwarfed by him and took a step backwards. It was as if the walls were closing in, her field of vision narrowing. She felt small and insignificant, in the shadow of his massive frame.

"If your father had taken you firmly in hand earlier, this would not be necessary now."

She watched the twitch in his cheek and was mesmerized by his furrowed brow. He was not messing about, and she knew her attitude was making him even more angry, but she didn't care. Her own blood was boiling. How *bloody* dare he talk to her like this? The thought of being physically punished for buying shoes was absurd. There was no way she was going to submit to this.

Barbara stood. She felt her jaw clench.

She watched as his grimace slowly transformed to a grin of pearly white teeth that left her feeling a bit like Little Red Riding Hood confronted by the wolf for the first time. His smile was disconcerting. It made her feel as if he knew something that she did not.

He stood there as immoveable as Mount Rushmore.

He flexed his shoulders. "So you are defying me?" His eyebrows rose in an impressive arch.

She said nothing but didn't break eye contact. The turmoil inside her grew. She wanted to fight him, yet she knew she didn't have the strength. She wanted to hit him and at the same time she wanted to cry and run for sanctuary. A warm flush hit her face while a cold tingle ran down her spine radiating to pins and needles in her fingers.

He folded his arms across his barrel like chest, his back ramrod straight, unyielding. "I did think of a third option, maybe it would suit you better."

He paused and Barbara racked her brain, searching for options of her own. There must be something. Maybe he would settle for a blowjob. The smile on his face sure hinted at that. She was sure it would pacify him for a while. She returned his smile, happy to have been let off the hook. She began to relax a little more thinking the storm was about to pass. A bullet dodged.

The expression on his face didn't change. "I could send you home to daddy. I am sure he would be delighted to have his little girl back.

Her heart sank into a bottomless pit of despair. Christ no! After all the fights with her father there was no way she could ever go back there to live.

"I'm sure he'd be delighted to be proved right. I'm sure he would be overjoyed to see you could not hack it in the real world." His words were cruel, yet she felt the truth in them.

A cold fear welled up inside her. She fidgeted with the hem of her skirt unsure what to say, searching for the words. A lump caught in her throat, she could not believe he was serious. He was talking about divorce, over shoes.

A flash of anger tingled through her fingers and she felt a warm flush across her cheek.

She tried to keep her composure. Maybe a little break would give him time to cool down and reconsider. Maybe it would make him a bit more reasonable.

"Give me the car keys." She spat the words like venom, fists clenched, expensive manicured nails pressing into her palms. A wave of cold washed over her again.

Alan threw his head back and laughed, "Not a chance! You leave here with what you brought to this house, a jewelry box, if you can carry it, and a shitty attitude. I suppose you might as well take these shoes. Better still walk home in them, I bet you won't get five yards."

She felt the finality of his words clear through her soul. She wiped her moistened palms on the soft fabric of her skirt. Would he seriously throw away their marriage for this?

She felt a pain in her chest. How could she have pushed him this far?

In an epiphany, she saw how trivial possessions were when weighed against her love for Alan. With this new insight glittering in her mind, she knew with clarity that she could not lose him; she would do anything to keep that from happening. He was her life, her bedrock and she could not see a world without him in it.

She felt her heart pounding in her chest as she looked up at him, looking for anything that would tell her she'd misunderstood, that he still loved her. There was nothing on his face that gave her the reassurance she so desperately needed.

The scenes of their marriage flashed through her mind, like snippets from a movie, each one bringing her closer to the dreadful, predictable end.

She saw by his chiseled, marble face, that he was not going to budge an inch. He was a man on the edge and she had pushed him there. She flinched, as a wave of guilt washed over her. She had really not meant to go this far. What she wanted above all else, was for him to make her his princess again. She felt herself wither, deflating like a balloon.

How could she leave? While her father never bitched about her spending he never gave her the feeling of being loved, protected, safe, nurtured, the way Alan had in their early marriage, before they had started to fight about how much money she spent. In walking away from Alan, she would walk away from everything she wanted.

She didn't want to leave and there was no way she could go back to the shop and return the shoes. She had run out of options. Her heart sank. The spanking was inevitable.

"God please Alan, let's not do this." A tone of pleading entered her voice. Her mind was an emotional briar patch, a tangle of mixed emotions. "Can't we just make up? I promise not to do this again."

Alan smirked, slowly shaking his head, "I remember you saying that last time. Oh yes, and the time before." He folded his arms across his chest.

"It will be different this time, I promise."

"Barbara, we have been here before." Alan looked at her,

his gaze met hers, pinning her, making her feel like a moth trapped in the glare of a bright light. "I am not doing this to be a horrible bastard." His fingertips stroked her cheek. "I love you. I really do want you to be happy. I just want you to be content with what we have."

She turned her head to the side, "And you think spanking me will make me content?" she asked, not understanding how a spanking would make her happy.

"Frankly, yes I do. You lack discipline and respect."

Not really having a reply for him she looked at the floor, the hollow void of shame enveloped her. Her head lowered in contemplation as she bowed to the inevitable.

"I take it that you are staying to face the music?" His expression was resolute. His tone was not of satisfaction. In fact, he seemed to be doing this reluctantly, rather than taking pleasure in it.

Maybe he *was* doing it for her own good.

She was aware of her own breathing, conscious the regular beat of her heart, as she remained silent looking at her feet. She felt a little sick, and her throat ached with the pent up need to cry, but no tears came.

His words came abruptly, cold and sharp, precise; his voice louder than it had been before. "Do you submit to corporal punishment?"

The sudden raising of tension, his unexpectedly harsh tone caught her off guard. She realized with horror that her bladder had let her down and she had wet herself. She closed her eyes in shame even though she knew the small leak remained her private shame.

"Yes." Her voice sounded small and dejected even to her own ears.

"You will address me as Sir during punishment." His voice was stern, as if he was talking to a member of his crew rather than his wife and it made her feel worthless and hollow.

"Yes Sir." She felt degraded and dirty, her wet panties making her feel even more childlike and unworthy of her husband.

"Strip, here in front of me please." His words were cool and matter-of-fact.

The simplicity of his words stunned her. There was a surreal quality, as if it was a dream and any moment she would wake up and find herself looking at her breakfast. But the stark reality was staring her in the face. Looking to his eyes, she saw Alan's jaw tighten and his brow furrow deeply. She wanted to comply, but she felt as if the wind had been taken from her sails. A million questions raced through her mind. How, in God's name, had it come to this? How could shopping have brought her to the edge of divorce?

"I want you to strip." His cold, clipped words dragged her from her own thoughts.

"Yes Sir." She felt a lump in her throat, felt the tears welling up, but fought them back. She caught the inside of her lip between her teeth. The sharpness kept her focused on what she had to do.

Her gaze climbed up his chest to meet his gaze, as she slipped off one shoe and then the other. They clattered noisily, as they fell onto the quarry-stone kitchen floor. Her gaze dropped as manicured fingernails slowly undid the buttons of her blouse. She looked up hoping to see some approval in his eyes, some softening, but she was disappointed to see only his steely resolve.

She shrugged off the blouse and laid it on the kitchen chair. She fought back the lump in her throat. She did not want him to see how lost she felt. She wanted to maintain at least that much dignity.

"Very nice." His words were simple but she thought she could hear a little of the ice melting.

Her teeth gripped her lip a little harder, tightening her resolve. She shivered and thumbed the bra strap from her shoulder as she reached around to release the clasp. She sensed his eyes burning into her naked flesh as she stood there feeling vulnerable and exposed. She lifted her arms to cover her breasts.

"I want to see you." His words sounded a little softer, which lifted her spirits a little.

Barbara looked up again, his face had softened slightly. His brow was less menacing and there was a hint of a smile, only a hint, but it made him look more approachable. She found it strangely arousing, almost as if she were an exotic dancer performing for a single client. She liked that he was giving her his full attention; it was almost like regaining a little dignity.

There was something erotic about the power he was exerting over her. In a funny way it was comforting that there was this physical consequence, that he was taking this step to curtail her spending. She also felt somewhat reassured that he cared enough to do this.

A host of sensations were coming to the surface. There was a melding of moisture as her clit throbbed to the same rhythm as her pulse. She found her breathing becoming faster, more labored. Looking down she could see her nipples were erect, aching to be fondled and sucked.

She turned her gaze back to Alan, as he unfolded his arms and placed them casually in his pockets and again she thought she could see the merest flicker of a smile. She wondered if he was enjoying this.

She let her gaze drop, feeling reassured by the bulge in his trousers. She liked the thought of his building hunger. She was relieved to see that his desire for her was undiminished.

Emboldened by the thought of his lust, she reached to the side of her skirt and slid down the zip, giving an extra wiggle as she shimmied and the black fabric pooled at her feet. If she put on a good enough show maybe that would be enough. It warmed her to think he might just wrap her in his arms and forget about the spanking.

She bent, gave her ass a seductive wiggle before picking up the skirt and placing it on the chair. As she straightened she turned to Alan. She watched as a knowing smile spread over his face. She searched for a reason beyond him enjoying the extra wiggle of her ass. Then, with a stab of horror it dawned on her that he could see her wet panties. In the passion of the moment, her slight accident had slipped her mind. Her cheeks flushed hot with embarrassment and she felt a rush of humiliation at the thought that her weakness had been exposed.

He seemed to be enjoying her shame. She could not really see the fascination; he had seen her with and without panties many times before. His gaze seemed transfixed on her crotch and the damp stain. Maybe it was the naughtiness of her wetting herself that had him so captivated.

She wondered what turned him on more, her humiliation or the prospect of beating her. She felt the curious persistent throb, between her legs. There was a heaviness deep in her feminine core, a persistent nag that would not be silenced.

She could not remember the last time she had been this aroused. She wanted him.

There was silence and she hesitated for just a moment, and thought of asking Alan if he would relent. Maybe he would be pacified by her mouth or a nice soft fuck. She saw his brow start to furrow again and felt her hope dwindle. She had seen him mellow, if just a little. She wanted her lover back and she saw him in his smile and warm eyes. She definitely did not want to see him freeze over again.

Without a word she hooked her thumbs into the waistband of her panties and slid them down unhooking them from her feet before placing the thin white cotton with her other clothes.

She stood erect and naked. The dimple in his cheek betrayed his broadening smile and the crow's feet at the corners of Alan's eyes showed his admiration of her body. She basked in the glow of his approval. It had been such a long time since she'd felt it and she felt warmed by it now. It felt as if her husband was beginning to return to her.

"Very good." He paused and there was a joyous tone in his voice. It was as if he was revelling in this moment of her submission. The brief praise made her glow, warming her like a sip of hot chocolate on a winter's day. "I want you to go to the bedroom. I will join you in a few minutes."

Barbara nodded. "Yes Sir."

The wait in their bedroom was unbearable. She stood trembling as the silence was broken by the tap of his leather soles landing on the hardwood stairs. The sound got louder as the footsteps approached slowly, menacingly. She wanted to run, scream, cry, beg him to give her another chance but fear had rooted her to the spot.

The floorboard creaked as he left the wood and stepped onto the bedroom carpet. She smelled his musky aftershave even before she saw him enter the room. Barbara lifted her head to look at him. His shirt was bright in the comparative gloom and he stood in front of her with his arms folded across his broad chest. She felt powerless, like a leaf on a breeze and totally at his mercy.

He stood motionless looking at her but saying nothing. She felt manipulated but unable to do anything about it. She stifled a sob as a tear finally broke free from the corner of her eye.

She felt its wet path as it slid down her cheek.

The silence stretched on as she realized that him making her wait this way was also part of his power over her. She shivered nervously convinced that he must be enjoying this.

The well of emotions whirled inside her each fighting for her attention. It was true she was scared, but she also felt exhilarated about the idea of being called to account and punished and it troubled her. What kind of woman *wanted* to be spanked?

Alan's presence loomed large by the bed, his silence, added to the tension. She had never felt this helpless, so completely without power. Daddy had been cross with her, yet even when she was a child he had not disciplined her with corporal punishment. He had made rules, but he had never made a rule that she had not been able to bend to suit herself. Alan was different and she had never really mastered the art of winding him around her fingers.

He broke the silence, his words slow, the sound of

controlled anger in his gravelly low voice.

"Barbara, we have talked before about your excessive spending and I thought I had made it plain that it was to stop. You have money to spend and I am not a tyrant. I want you to be happy." His words trailed off.

If he wanted to make her happy why the punishment? Why not simply stop bitching about the money? That would make her very happy.

There must have been something in her face that gave her thoughts away.

"I can see you are confused. Happiness is not about material things." He sighed. "I want to teach you that there is more to life than simply acquiring stuff. There is a joy in contentment, in restraint, in the simple things in life."

Alan's words made her feel bad about spending money, as if there was something foul and dirty about it. But there was an addictive quality to having that kind of power. It made her feel like she had with Alan at the beginning, so wanted, so needed. She loved the way the sales people followed her around. It made her feel special.

Why wouldn't Alan show her that kind of attention?

"I can see that you don't believe me." He inclined his head toward her, inviting her to speak.

She looked hard for the right words, but none came easily, "I don't know... There is something missing. I feel lonely. When I feel that way I shop. I can't explain it."

Alan looked serious. "I am trying to understand Barbara. I really do want you to be happy but I know that shopping is not the answer. Spending money on things we don't need is disrespectful." His expression was more hurt than angry.

It was something that until now she hadn't truly considered. She knew that her actions angered him, but she hadn't realized that they hurt him.

Alan came over to her and softly stroked her hair as he talked. "I feel I have to lay down the law, and when I do you ignore me. What am I supposed to do with you? I have tried everything. Reasoning with you, arguing with you, even cutting up the credit card and yet nothing I say makes a scrap of difference. That is why I think a physical correction is necessary. I think it will get the message across."

Her heart sank, dread settling over her like a heavy dark fog that clogged her throat and squeezed her chest making it hard to get her thoughts into words. She was aware of the distance that had grown between them. She felt so sad that it had come to this. She wanted to be a good wife, but when they fought, or when Alan was away at sea the loneliness crept into her soul crowding out her good intentions.

She looked into her husband's eyes, as she stood there, stripped naked before him. It was not just that she was naked, she felt her soul exposed.

She looked up at him and saw the pained expression in his eyes. Her chest ached as she spoke. "I want to be happy too." She sighed, enjoying the soothing touch of his hand as he stroked her hair. "I want you to be happy, and I want you to be happy with me." Her voice cracked and she stifled a sob wondering if that were possible now. "I want it to be like it was in the beginning. I want you to be proud of me again."

The tension that had furrowed his brow had dissolved, his soft smile and warm eyes had returned. Alan wrapped his arms around her, covering her naked flesh with his body. It felt like coming home after a long trip away as she melted into his chest, felt his warm breath on her hair.

"I am so proud of you." He whispered the words, his mind catching on the things that made him proudest. He loved her dedication to organizations that helped the poor and the sick. He admired her tenacity. He'd never seen her let financial obstacles stand in the way when it came to one of her charities. He'd seen her cajole and chide her way through her parent's circle of acquaintances getting them to give time and money to support one of her charities. He stroked her cheek. He was proud of her. Damned proud.

"I love you. I always have and I always will, but that doesn't mean that I am happy about $1500 shoes."

He truly felt that this was a turning point, though he debated whether he should spank her, wondering if it would sour the reconciliation that had happened between them.

Even so he wanted to cement their newfound commitment in a very physical way. He didn't want to hurt her but he knew from deep down inside that a physical punishment would make their union even stronger. A line needed to be drawn.

He took in a deep breath and let it out slowly. His big hands took her shoulders, holding her so their eyes met. "I do love you and I do want to make everything right between us. But that said, retail therapy is not the answer." He ran his fingers through her hair, then stroked down her cheek. He enjoyed the feel of her soft skin as he took hold of her chin and lifted her gaze to meet his. "There is a lesson to be learned and the shoes have to be paid for, one way or another." His voice trailed off. There was a hint of resolute determination in it. "I am wanting to draw a line under this incident so that we can move on."

Barbara gave him a half smile. Although she was complying he could sense her uneasiness with the idea.

"I think this needs to be done. Are you willing to submit?"

She heard no malice in his voice, just the tone of a task that had to be done.

"Yes Sir," her voice sounded shaky even to her own ears.

"Freely? And willingly?"

The tremble that worked through her made her voice wobble. "Yes Sir."

She didn't *want* him to spank her, but she felt there was no alternative. She wanted to get her life back to normal, put the past behind and start over and if this was the way she would do whatever it took to set things right. "I will do whatever you ask, of my own free will."

"Good girl, I am pleased that you will submit." She felt the warmth of his hand, as he stroked her cheek softly, reassuring her of the need for this action. "I know you are reluctant; this is your first time. I know you are scared because you don't know what is going to happen, but I hope you will come to see that this is for your own good."

Although his words sounded sincere, she could not reconcile in her own mind, the two sides of the coin, his words of love and his need to inflict punishment. But then again she could not tie together why the thought of this scared her and aroused her at the same time. Maybe it was the same for him.

She looked up for a moment and saw him standing there, menacing, totally in control. In his hands she saw he was holding a length of pink rope and the riding crop.

Alan straightened himself to his full height, feeling the muscles in his back flex, "So my pet, with this punishment we have a new start. The slate wiped clean."

He looked down at Barbara. Her head was lowered in natural submission, yet there was a part of her that still seemed strong and defiant. Despite the disobedience there was something about her strength he admired. He also felt that in some way he had played his part in this situation. If he had not been so indulgent in their early days together, if he had been clear about what he wanted in the first place, shown her more attention, then maybe it would not have gone this far.

"Look up please." His gaze caught hers. He saw the worry in her chocolaty brown eyes and felt a wave of concern that this was too much.

"I know this is hard for you, but it is for the best." He saw her tremble as she watched him place the crop on the bed. Her lip quivered as he picked up the pink silk rope and stretched a section of the cord between his clenched fists.

He gestured to the bedroom dressing stool in the middle of the bedroom. "I want you to lay over the stool please."

She gave him an apprehensive sideways glance.

He took a step back to give her room to position herself. He allowed himself a smile as he watched with satisfaction and a sense of pride as she complied with his instruction.

He watched as her soft breasts pushed against the velvety

covering on the small backless stool, trying to imagine how the soft material felt against her smooth skin. His dexterous fingers tied her to the stool with the pink silk rope. He hoped in time the restraints would not be necessary, but for the first time he did not want her wriggling about. His eyes wandered over her, apprehensively. She looked so submissive and he found her vulnerability arousing, yet he was aware of the responsibility that weighed on his shoulders.

Holding the riding crop at either end he flexed the shaft in his hands. It was pleasingly subtle. He remembered the excitement of finding the crop and the thrill the first time he swiped the air with it. He loved the swish, loved the way the tightly bound thin strips of leather felt in his hand. Feeling it now he recalled practicing with it first on a pillow and then on his hand. Over time he had progressed to his own thigh. The thought of the sting still made his thigh ache.

Alan viciously swiped at the air with the crop, loving both the sound it made and the way it made her twitch and flinch in anticipation of a swipe landing on her. "Now my pet, it is time to answer for your misdemeanors."

He liked the fact she was expecting the worst, but he felt he could not use the crop, not this first time anyway. He considered it a step too far too soon.

He shook the tension out of his shoulders and took up a pose, readying himself before he struck. The first strike was with the flat of his hand on her right ass cheek. He was surprised at the sting in his own hand but he liked the satisfying sound of flesh on flesh and the heat that radiated through his own palm.

She let out a little yelp, he guessed more out of surprise than any pain or discomfort. He hadn't struck that hard. He wanted to start slowly, testing how she would react to his hand striking her bottom.

He enjoyed the idea of surprising her, never really letting her know what was going to happen next. He landed a second spank on her other cheek. He liked the feeling of her hot skin on his hot hand.

His second spank landing was accompanied by her letting out a gasp and then a low whimper.

He lifted his palm and took the time to observe with pride the two hand prints on her peachy skin. His penis twitched in the tight confines of his pants. A third spank landed with a juicy slap, reddening her skin further and making Barbara suck in a breath. With the fourth spank, her skin began to glow a pleasing pink.

He found that as the color deepened, his penis got harder. After all the time of feeling impotent, unable to tame her he finally felt in control. .

"Please Sir!" Her voice was ragged. "Pleeeeeease, no more"

He ignored her plea and with each spank he felt more spiritually uplifted more in charge of the situation.

His hand landed again, she wriggled against her bonds "Please, Sir... Please stop... Please..."

The spanking was surely not hard enough to injure her, though he expected it stung. He did not want to hurt her, but he did want to drive home the point, remind her who was in charge. He kept a mental note of the number of strikes. Seven and her bottom was a cherry pink. He felt her tremble beneath him, she wriggled and resisted. It was a wonderful feeling to exercise this level of control and restraint.

"Sir! It hurts Sir! I promise to be good."

Alan again, assessed the intensity of his swats and considered them strong enough to sting, but not to injure her, yet she continued to plead for mercy. He determined that if the spanking was to do any good, it should be a lesson that would be remembered.

As Alan landed the ninth, he paid special attention to not striking on any of the previous marks, his goal was to get an even shade, from the tops of her thighs to the top of her buttocks.

"Sir, please, I won't do it again."

More spanks fell and although she still pleaded and

struggled, it seemed to him that her struggles had lost some of their intensity.

Alan's heart pounded in his chest, his breath felt tight in his throat. He noticed a bead of sweat trickle down his brow. Until then he had not considered how much physical effort he was expending. He enjoyed the buzzy feeling it gave him, that endorphin rush urged him on. The next spank was a tad harder.

Barbara let out a little squeal, it didn't sound like pain, more like she was enjoying it, or at least was resigned to it.

Urged on, he felt a sweet ache in his groin. His hand adjusted his penis in an attempt to make himself more comfortable. He could see that he was not the only one to be receiving pleasure from the spanking. He noticed a dribble of sweet nectar moistening her nether lips. The small mewing noises she made seemed now to be more the moans of pleasure. It pleased him to think this was not one sided. He stopped spanking and noticed his hand ached. He imagined it must be the same for her ass. He slowly ran a finger along her labia. She moaned and he felt her push back. She really was enjoying this. He slipped his moist finger inside and softly stroked in and out.

"How are you doing?"

Her voice was hesitant. "I am fine Sir." Her hips pushing back and forth showed how very turned on she was. She certainly didn't seem to be any worse for this experience, in fact quite the contrary she actually seemed to be enjoying it. He looked at her reddening bottom. He considered stopping there and taking her from behind, picturing himself buried inside her, his stomach pushed tight to her warm bottom. The idea was very potent, the position very dominant, he'd be truly in the driving seat. He wanted her but decided to wait, resisting the urge for instant gratification.

"How do you feel?" he asked, hoping the warmth of his feelings came out in his voice.

"I feel fine Sir." Her voice sounded more confident now.

"I think you like it…the spanking, not my finger." She said nothing but wiggled her hips and gave him a little smile as she looked over her shoulder. "Do you want more?" He paused. "Pain then pleasure?"

"Yes Sir," she answered, her voice low and seductive.

"Pain then pleasure?"

"Yes Sir," she repeated, her voice husky with need.

The sound of her voice filled with desire, fueled his own need. He wanted her more now than any time he could remember. It took all his willpower not to make love to her then and there. As he withdrew his finger, she let out a little whine, obviously missing the digit. He wiped the wetness on the warmed reddened skin of her ass. He landed another affectionate spank sweetly on her left cheek.

She missed the feel of his hand when it stopped spanking. She craved Alan's attention. She shuddered when she felt his fingers touch her sensitive, swollen labia, hungered for him to take her, to possess her.

"How does my little girl like this?" His voice was warm with affection.

She couldn't manage more than a mew of contentment. Loving the feeling of his strong dominant fingers as he slowly fondled her clit. The sensation was driving her wild, it was like pins and needles playing on her skin, yet at the same time being stroked with a piece of silk. His finger was at the entrance of her treasure and she could not resist the urge to push back, wantonly impaling herself onto his erect digit.

"Yes, my girl, is hungry, isn't she?" His tone encouraged her.

"Hmmmm, yes Sir… God yes…" She was sopping wet, and the throb in her clit was driving her crazy. She desperately wanted to cum and she knew he was deliberately denying her orgasm.

"Does my little girl want more?" There was a tease in his voice.

"Mmm… Please Sir… I'll do anything Sir… Please Sir…" She would joyfully agree to anything, just so long as he wouldn't stop. She felt the fire growing inside her and felt herself close to the edge. Just a little further and she would surrender to her building orgasm.

Suddenly the sensations stopped and the finger was removed, her pleasure denied.

"Sir?" There was desperation in her voice.

"Silence… Not a word." His words were commanding.

She stayed quiet, but God! What was he doing? He'd stopped! She wanted to plead, beg, but there was no doubt that he was in command. She felt his finger, slick with her wetness, wipe over her bottom. The moisture cooled her ass cheek.

She lay there alone with her thoughts, physically empty, hungry and wanting, waiting, at his mercy, consumed with a mix of excitement and apprehension.

The first thing Barbara knew of the change from his hand to the crop, was the bee sting on her ass. She felt the electricity buzz through her and the fire was stoked again.

Another sting bit. She loved the way he made her feel. It was curiously liberating handing the control to Alan.

Barbara let out a little gasp as the third swat of the crop landed and her buttocks clenched, sending little electric shock waves through her body. She should hate this, yet she didn't. She felt surprisingly comforted by the restraints, it was like being healed, forgiven. What was it Alan had said, the slate wiped clean?

She was calmed by the mixture of feelings, pleasure and pain in equal measure. She loved the tingly feeling in her bottom and the insistent throb of her clit as the crop bit. The initial discomfort and humiliation had given way to a warm throb deep in her center. The warmth had grown to a fire that spread though her body.

It seemed inappropriate to actually enjoy corporal punishment. Yet there it was, she found it curiously pleasurable to submit to this. She welcomed the sweet and sour, the sugar dissolving in the vinegar, the subtle mixture of pain and pleasure.

Another bee stung her tender ass. She felt intoxicated. Thoughts wandered into her mind in the hazy way they do after couple of glasses of wine. Had she bought the shoes to deliberately provoke him?

Of course she had never had this in mind. She had never seen Alan in quite this way before, but she had been aware of his power, his intransigence and how much his assertiveness turned her on.

Another sting of the crop and she felt the sparks of desire fly. Her pubis found the edge of the stool. Instinctively she ground her mound on it; she felt the hard edge contrasting with the soft fabric. This newly added stimulation was just enough to get her right on the edge, but not quite enough to make her tumble into the abyss of the orgasm she so desperately needed. She tried to push harder but the promised land she craved eluded her.

A cool breeze caught the trickle of liquid on her inner thigh. Her breath caught in her throat as the bite of another crop strike caught her between her cheeks. Her body was alive as the electric sparks flew once more.

Rolling waves of pleasure set up a slow penetrating rhythm deep in her centre, contrasting with the sharp spikes the crop burnt into her flesh. The rhythm pushed her closer and closer to the cliff edge. She felt the pins and needles in her skin, the rough and smooth the threshold of climax. She surrendered herself totally to him as she toppled over the invisible edge into the pit of carnal lust.

She swooned, as the first vinegary tingles washed over her. The bitter sweet waves tingled, from the tips of her fingers to the tips of her toes. She was lost in a sensory overload that cascaded over her. Muscles clenched and relaxed in throbbing cascades of sensation. She felt the hardness of her teeth clench on the softness of her lower lip. A wash of colors sounds and textures filled her mind. Soft, hard, sweet, bitter. The world became a timeless place. An explosion that burned white hot and cool all at the same time. She felt as if she was melting away. Bliss enveloped her in warm waves.

Alan felt himself breathing heavily. There was an ache in his arm and the exertion had soaked his shirt with perspiration. For now at least he regarded the tigress within her had been tamed. He felt contented and centered. He wanted to hold the lady he loved. Then he wanted to make long slow love to her, to make her his again. He wanted her to see him as the giver of pleasure, as well as pain. He wanted to be everything to her. Protector and Master.

He looked at her flaccid over the stool and worried that he had gone too far this first time. Had he been too rough? Had he hurt her? His mind bubbled with questions as he untied her. Through his concern he looked at her punished bottom and took a certain pride in the accuracy of the pattern of welts on her ass. The design was beginning to spread and merge, as the bruises came out, joining together in a kaleidoscope of colors.

He spread out his favorite bathroom towel on the bed to protect the Egyptian cotton sheets, lifted her onto the towel and softly massaged oil into her bottom. She lay passively, as he enjoyed the feel of her peachy skin reddened and heated by his chastisement. He felt immensely proud that she had bourn the punishment without verbal complaint. His fingers made patterns in the oil that soothed his hand which had been reddened by the spanking.

With her surrender to him, he felt that this would be a new beginning for them, or at least he hoped so. Maybe the spankings would be a feature of their love making. For the moment he was content to be with her, so close, so together.

The world slowly returned to Barbara. Her mind was fuzzy. Like waking from a dream, realities began to dawn on her. She was no longer on the floor, tied. Alan must have untied her and carried her to the bed without her realizing it. She was laying face down on a fluffy towel and he was affectionately massaging a soothing and sweet smelling balm into her tender, punished flesh.

She knew, as she had right at the start, that she loved Alan with all her heart. He was her rock, the man that provided all the love and structure she could possibly need. The chastisement really would be a turning point…good for her…good for them. He had been right all along.

Cara Bristol

Intimate Submission

www.blackvelvetseductions.com

Intimate Submission

Jamie Douglass paused outside the offices of Reese Thomas Enterprises and tugged at her too-short and overly-tight black skirt, regretting her choice of attire. She'd worn her favorite mini and her highest heels because today she needed the confidence they usually afforded her.

All of her hopes hinged on the outcome of this job interview. Since graduating from college three years ago with a bachelor's in business, she'd worked as a project manager for a software development company. When the economy took a turn for the worse, her boss, a teddy bear of a man, had been forced to let her go. He'd been as upset as she was—almost. She'd sent out scores of résumés, but the only one that resulted in a call was the one to Reese Thomas Enterprises.

Assistant needed to handle special assignments for hard-driven, intense executive of business consulting firm. Must be able to multi-task, operate out-of-the-box, push the envelope, yet thrive on discipline. Desire motivated, responsive individual willing to perform under pressure in return for exceptional reward and excellent benefits.

As it turned out, her former boss knew the company's chief executive and founder and put in a good word for her. To Jamie, he offered a pep talk—of sorts.

"If Reese seems hard and stern, it's because he is. But he's also uncompromisingly fair. He demands a hundred and ten percent, but he gives the same. Don't let him scare you. You're a terrific asset to any company, and I'm certain you two will hit it off. You're perfect for him."

Poised on the threshold with her old boss's words ringing in her ears, Jamie's doubts caused her stomach to churn. How could she satisfy someone who expected a hundred and ten percent? Taking a deep breath, she pushed open the door and stepped inside.

Her feet sank into lush, thick carpeting as she surveyed the rich mahogany furniture and the original art adorning the walls. A professionally-coiffed and uber-efficient-looking receptionist was retrieving her purse from a drawer in her L-shaped marble-topped desk.

She smiled at Jamie's approach. "May I help you?" She set her purse on the credenza.

"I'm Jamie Douglass. I have a twelve o'clock appointment with Reese Thomas."

The secretary arched one eyebrow. "Yes, of course." She nodded and picked up the phone. "I'll let her know."

The receptionist looked at Jamie. "His conference call is running longer than expected. Please take a seat. He'll be with you shortly. If you'll excuse me, I was on my way to lunch."

Jamie tugged at her skirt again before perching on a hand-tooled leather sofa. She pressed her legs together and kept her posture straight, wanting to make a good first impression.

The minutes ticked by. Five. Ten. Fifteen. As she waited, her nervousness grew. By the time the door opened and a man emerged, Jamie's flip-flopping stomach had mastered the cha-cha and two other dances.

Piercing eyes zeroed in on her. "Are you here for the job interview?" His raspy, commanding tone sent a shiver up her spine.

"Yes, sir," she answered automatically. She rose as he approached, craning her neck to see his face. "I'm Jamie Douglass."

His unfriendly features appeared carved out of stone. Although it was only midday, a new beard shadowed his jaw. His chin was square, his mouth firm, but it was his eyes that caused her stomach to flutter with trepidation. Flinty gray, they betrayed no emotion, only impassive disregard. No one would dare call him handsome. Deadly attractive, brutally sexy, but never handsome. Despite her nerves, her body quivered in response to his rugged masculinity.

"Reese Thomas?" She extended her hand courageously.

"Reese Nichols," he corrected as he shook her hand with an aggressive grip. He had strong hands, broad fingers. "Thomas was my father. I named the company after myself and my father."

Stupid! She cursed silently as heat flooded her face. Why hadn't she checked that out? "Of course," she forced out an answer. "I apologize."

This close she could smell the soap he used and a wholly masculine scent that was all his own. His gaze swept over her, assessing and appraising, as if to glean from her demeanor whether she could handle the job. She felt his scrutiny as a palpable thing, stroking her from head to toe. Her ears buzzed. Her stomach fluttered as her pussy surged with wetness and her nipples started to salute. Jamie's heart thumped in horror as desire hit her like a bullet train at rush hour. Never in her twenty-five years had she experienced such a strong reaction to a man.

She didn't want to feel this way about a stranger, a potential employer no less, and judging from his shuttered expression, her desire was one-sided, so why did she feel abandoned when he released her hand?

"You were on time," he said. His voice sounded as rough as his beard would be grazing over her breast, before sliding lower…

S*top it!* She suppressed the erotic images that flooded her mind.

She moistened her dry lips. "Yes, sir."

***

Reese stifled a curse. Two words. The two simple words spoken by a woman with the voice of a phone sex operator shot straight to his cock. *Yes, sir. Fuck me harder, sir*, Reese imagined her pleading. Until this moment, he hadn't realized how much he enjoyed being called sir.

Based on his college buddy's glowing recommendation, he'd been expecting a middle-aged, sexless paragon. But when he had opened his office door, her sexuality had decked him like a sucker punch. She'd straightened her shoulders and stiffened her spine, but her bravado couldn't mask the sexy-as-hell vulnerability in her brown eyes, nor the faint trembling of her rosy mouth designed by God for sucking cock.

She'd attempted to subdue her sexuality by raking her hair into a tight coil and donning a sharply-tailored jacket to cover the swell of her breasts, but she had betrayed her nature by donning fuck-me shoes. Her stilettos made her legs a mile long, gave sway to her walk, and thrust out her chest. God, he loved fuck-me shoes.

She was a captivating mix of innocence and wantonness. His gut told him that under the right man's hands—*his*—her ass in particular, and her sexuality in general, would blossom like a hothouse rose. He didn't want to hire her; he wanted to paddle her ass and then fuck her every which way to Monday and it was only Friday.

Reese gestured for her to precede him. "After you, Ms. Douglass."

"It's Miss Douglass, sir."

Reese shut the office door behind them and noticed that Jamie jumped a little. "So you're not one of those hard-core feminist types?" He couldn't resist teasing her.

She turned to face him, her chin raised to meet the challenge. "Certainly I believe a woman ought to use her abilities to her greatest potential, but I am not a man."

Thank God, for that, Reese thought. "Have a seat." He gestured toward a wooden club chair fronting his desk. "May I call you Jamie?"

"Yes, sir," she answered, and another shock ricocheted through his hardening cock.

He took his own seat, noting that her eyes were riveted on his desk. He glanced at the gleaming surface and had the urge to leap over the barrier and bend her over the polished wood.

She raised her gaze to meet his, and he watched as her cheeks turned rosy. He wondered what hidden thoughts had brought the color to her face and if those thoughts had anything to do with the hard nipples beading through her lightweight jacket. Her curvy ass would probably turn as pretty a pink as her face if he spanked her. His rock hard cock urged him to find out.

At thirty-seven, Reese was still searching for the right woman to warm his heart and his bed. He'd long ago recognized his dominant nature and his need to control, but he didn't want a doormat. He'd dated a few submissives, but they'd lacked spunk. Other women played along, but it wasn't their nature to submit. He desired fire and spice with his sugar, someone a little shy, yet adventurous under his guiding hand. A woman who *was* submissive, but also passionate and sassy.

Jamie's part professional, part sex-kitten attire and her deferential responses seemed to indicate she might be that woman. Reese's gut told him she was the one. He trusted his gut. It was never wrong.

Reese held her gaze and leaned forward. "I need to make something perfectly clear before we proceed. I'm looking for someone who can think for herself, who isn't afraid to try new things, but who knows my word is final. I'm demanding, but fair. I have high expectations. Satisfy me and you'll be rewarded."

He paused. "Fail, and there are consequences for that, too."

***

Jamie's breath caught in her throat as her cunt spasmed. He was talking about the job, for Chrissakes! What was wrong with her that she inferred lewdness in his words, his tone?

"Jamie?" His eyes narrowed.

"I understand."

"So you think you perform well under firm discipline?"

Jamie lifted her chin, faking confidence. "I thrive on it, sir."

"You have no problem submitting to authority?" Reese leaned back in his chair. He undid the button of his jacket, and Jamie's eyes were drawn to the way his near-black suit and crisp white shirt molded the lines of his muscular body. Desire fluttered in her stomach and to quell it, she dropped her gaze and focused on his desk.

Bad move. Instantly she pictured him bending her over the polished surface as he drove into her from behind. Jamie bit her lip to suppress a moan.

She forced herself to focus on his question. It was something about submitting to authority. That was it. Did she have trouble doing what she was told? "No sir," she answered carefully. Why did his eyes flash every time she said, 'Yes, sir,' or 'No, sir'? "I understand this is a supportive role. In my last position as a project manager—"

The interview passed in a blur. When she thought about it afterwards, she couldn't recall what Reese had asked or how she'd answered, only that she had ached with sexual arousal

At the conclusion of the interview, she stood up on quivering legs. She clamped them together in a futile attempt to control the trembling and halt the flow of moisture from her creaming pussy. Her nipples hurt. "Thank you for the opportunity," she said, extending her hand as Reese rounded the desk.

Sexual energy jolted through her as he clasped it, but she forced herself to concentrate. She wet her lips. "Could…could you tell me when you expect to make a decision?"

"I've already made it." His shuttered expression told her he wasn't yet going to share it with her. He exerted a subtle pressure to pull her closer to him before releasing her hand. "Have lunch with me." It wasn't a request.

Run! Her rational mind screamed.

"Yes," she agreed, then added, sir."

"Do you know what happens to little girls who play with fire, Jamie?" he asked in a low tone.

She tossed her head. "They get burned?"

"They get spanked."

Jamie stifled a gasp, unable to believe what she'd heard – or her body's traitorous response. Her pussy released a new surge of moisture and her clit pulsed. Her limbs felt rubbery. But he was just joking…flirting. Right?

Her stomach fluttered as she read the serious intent on his face. He really *would* spank her. No one had ever laid a hand on her. Her gaze dropped to his hands at his sides, hard and masculine, his fingers long and broad. She felt her eyes widen more as she noticed the erection tenting his slacks.

"Let's go to lunch, Jamie," Reese rasped.

This was insane. She'd never reacted so strongly to anyone. What if by some miracle he offered her the job? She couldn't work here! She shouldn't even have lunch with him!

"Yes." She nodded.

Reese guided her out of his office with a possessive hand on the small of her back. It burned through two layers of clothing to her flesh, leaving her to wonder if she would find a branded handprint on her skin. He did not release her once they exited the building, but maintained contact as if she might bolt.

If she had any sense, she would. She had a hunch Reese would demand more than she'd ever considered giving to anyone. He would allow no holding back, no offering half measures, no keeping a part of herself inviolate and private.

Even though her rational mind urged her to flee, her painfully aroused body and thumping heart wouldn't let her. Something about him drew her to him, ignited a yearning deep within that she sensed only he could fulfill.

He led her to his vehicle, a low-slung, two-seater sports car, made for speed and power, but not for graceful entry while wearing heels and a micro-mini skirt. Jamie did her best, but her skirt rode even higher up her thighs. Once again, she cursed her clothing choice.

The car's interior was small and tight and seemed smaller still when Reese folded himself into the driver's seat and shut the door. She felt the heat emanating from his body and caught his masculine scent. It mingled with the richness of leather and, to her embarrassment, the not-so-faint musk of her arousal.

He turned to her, his gaze lingering on her mouth before shifting to her eyes. "Buckle up," he said.

Her fingers fumbled over the seat belt, and he reached across her body to pull the strap and slip it into the buckle. She sucked in her breath at his closeness. Though he never actually made contact with her body, she was sharply, shamefully aware of him.

He handled the powerful car expertly, driving neither too fast nor too slow to the restaurant, an intimate, swanky place she had always wanted to try, but could never afford. The service was impeccable, the waiters efficient but unobtrusive, knowing when to appear, when to disappear. The food, she supposed, was excellent, though she tasted little of what she ate.

She discovered Reese had a light side, and he teased her to laughter. But the lightness didn't eliminate her roiling sexual need, or the hunger that flashed in his flinty eyes. They had finished lunch, and Jamie had declined dessert when Reese pulled out his cell phone.

Her heart stopped beating as she listened to him call his office and cancel his appointments for the remainder of the day. "You're not going to hire me, are you?" She asked when he hung up.

"No, Jamie," His tone was even as if he were discussing the meal they'd just eaten. "I'm going to spank your pretty little ass until it's rosy pink, and then I'm going to fuck you senseless."

***

"Where are we going?" Jamie asked as he seated her in his car.

He shut her door and rounded the vehicle, lowering himself into the leather driver's seat. He glanced at her. "I have a condo in the city."

"Oh." Jamie couldn't believe she was doing this. She was going to let this man fuck her, a man she'd known less than a few hours. Her rational, reasonable, cautious mind rebelled, but her body and that inexplicable, nameless yearning overrode its concerns. Sexual desire coiled within her so tightly, she hurt. She'd never wanted a man so much in her entire life.

Reese's "condo" turned out to be a high-rise penthouse with a spectacular view of the city skyline through its floor-to-ceiling windows. It was furnished with modern, masculine furniture and hard sleek surfaces that mirrored the hardness of the owner. She had only a moment to take it all in because Reese was there, behind her, turning her in his arms.

The muscles of his face were corded and taut, his eyes almost savage. The comments he'd made in the interview—discipline, submission, reward, punishment—replayed in her mind, and her heartbeat quickened.

Kiss me! She wanted to scream, yet some inner wisdom held her tongue, knowing she needed to wait for his lead.

"Would you like a glass of wine? Champagne?" he asked. His words were civilized, his tone polite. It was her imagination that concocted a more dangerous current beneath the surface.

She shook her head. She was drunk enough on Reese.

"Take off your jacket." No "please," no "if you like," and there was no mistaking the command in his tone now. She should have been outraged, should have rebelled on principle, but instead she felt a wet warmth between her legs and her nipples tighten.

Jamie's fingers fumbled over the buttons of her lightweight black blazer, but she got it undone and slipped it off her shoulders. She tossed her jacket onto a nearby chair with a forced casualness. A blaze of lust ignited in Reese's eyes, but he made no move to touch her. "Now, the rest of your clothes."

Jamie's lips parted. He hadn't even kissed her yet! "But—" She broke off her protest at the warning in his eyes.

Undressing with a lover had always just happened; it had never been approached with such deliberation. And never had she done it while he stood fully clothed, as if she were entertaining him with a private strip show. Her head bowed and she pulled off her camisole, the silk sliding over the tips of her aching breasts. The wisp of fabric joined the jacket. She had, she thought, rather average breasts with rosy brown areolas and long nipples, especially when excited to hardness as they were now. She wondered what Reese thought, but couldn't bring herself to peek at his face.

Every sense seemed to be heightened. She could hear her clothing sliding against her skin as she removed it, feel the brush of fabric like a stranger's touch. Her breathing sounded loud in her ears. She could smell the earthy scent of him and her own arousal mingling. Her stomach churned as nervousness and desire warred within her. Her fingers fumbled with the zipper on her skirt, before managing to slide it down to permit the skirt to pool at her feet. She hesitated, then hooked her thumbs into the waistband of her lacy black thong and pulled it off, revealing neatly trimmed dark curls.

She was naked now except for her stilettos. Uncertain what to do about those, she decided to leave them on. Besides, she needed the extra height to counter Reese's towering presence. Steeling her courage, she lifted her chin and met his eyes.

In them she saw raw carnality but also approval. She realized his order for her to disrobe had been a test, and she'd passed. She should have been annoyed, but instead felt curiously gratified that she'd pleased him.

Reese reached out to tilt her head back. Jamie's eyes closed as his mouth took possession of hers. His lips were smooth, yet firm, his stubbled jaw deliciously abrasive against her face.

He didn't coax, but commanded a response, and she responded with fervor, her tongue twining with his, her teeth nipping at his lips, her body yielding against his. Her limbs felt loose and boneless, her core flooded with liquid heat.

He released the clip in her French twist, sending her hair cascading over her shoulders to mid-back. A growl rumbled in his chest as his hands slid down her body to grip her ass cheeks and pull her against his erection. He pressed hard and thick against her abdomen, the length of him seeming to go on forever. Her pussy clenched and wept at the size of him.

Her nipples ached for his touch and he must have read her mind because he covered her breasts, kneading the mounds before capturing the tips between his thumbs and forefingers. Sensation shot through her, a tormenting, gnawing ache. He played with the pebbled buds, rolling and pinching. It was too much to take and yet not enough. Jamie stifled a moan, arching her back.

Reese broke off the kiss. As he lifted her into his arms and carried her through the condo, she realized she was being swept away not only by his physical strength and commanding presence but also by her own churning emotions. She was careening down a Category Five rapid on a roiling river. All she could do was cling to him and hang on.

Like the living area, the bedroom appeared even more expansive because of the large windows that opened it to the sky. But the enormous bed, draped with a faux fur leopard cover, captured her attention. Jamie floated on a cloud of lust as Reese set her on her feet. His head bent and he seized one aching nipple in his mouth. Satisfaction shot through her from the tip of her breast to her womb. Her fists curled in his thick hair. His tongue swirled around the bud, teasing it, before his mouth closed tighter and he tugged it to even greater hardness. Curls of pleasure danced along her nerve endings. His teeth bit into her, and her pleasure spiked to a sharp, demanding hunger. She pressed against him, craving more.

His mouth shifted to the other breast, and his hand to her

mound, toying with her curls before slipping into her slit.

Reese growled triumphantly. "I knew you were wet for me. I could smell your pussy in my office, in my car."

His thumb honed in on her clit as two fingers slipped inside her. She moved against his hand, trying to take him deeper. He nipped hard on one distended bud, which would have driven Jamie over the edge had he not released her clit and pussy. He gently propelled her onto the bed, so she was lying flat. He pulled off her shoes and pressed her thighs apart. "Spread your legs. I want to see you," he said.

Lying on his bed, spread before him, she felt onstage at top of the world, vulnerable and exposed—yet more turned on than she'd ever been in her life. She stifled fears about getting involved with a man who demanded not only her body but submission, too.

"You're so beautiful." Reese's approval pierced her with satisfaction. With cool, controlled movements, he stripped off his suit coat and draped it over a chair. His tie, shirt and slacks followed. As he divested himself of his clothing, he watched her.

She stifled a gasp when he slipped off his shorts. Hugely massive, his cock jutted out from a base of black swirls and large balls. A plum-sized head crowned the long, thick shaft.

She made a noise in her throat, and Reese moved closer to the bed. "Get on your knees."

She obeyed. It never occurred to her not to.

Satisfaction flashed in his gaze. He reached out and stroked her hair before winding his fingers through the strands. "You want to suck my cock, don't you?"

Jamie's lips parted. "Yes…sir."

He applied gentle, but firm downward pressure on her head and guided his cock to her lips.

Opening her mouth, she engulfed the massive crown. Her fingers wrapped around his rod, his shaft so thick her fingers didn't meet. Heat seared her palm as she stroked his cock. She licked at the pre-come slickening the smooth head, savoring the taste and feel of him. Trailing down his shaft with her lips and tongue, she teased his balls and then returned to the head. She took him inside her mouth until he touched the back of her throat, swallowed and took more of him. Her head bobbed, her fingers stroking, eagerly working him.

His breathing grew ragged and he rolled her nipples as she sucked him. She realized he was showing her what he wanted done to him by how he played with her nipples. When he tugged gently, she should stroke him lightly. When he tugged forcefully, she should suck him hard. She loved the feel, the taste of him, wanted to mark herself with his masculine scent.

He pulled away abruptly, but before she could protest, turned her around, and put her on her hands and knees, her ass jutting out, her breasts dangling, her pussy in full view. Jamie glanced at the bare windows and a lurid thrill skittered through her. This high in the sky no one could see them, but the exposure intensified her desire.

His hands caressed the smooth globes of her bottom, smoothing over the flesh. "Your ass is cool, Jamie. Do you think I should warm it up? Make it burn?"

Her mind whirled. She'd never been spanked before. Did she really want him to? What if she didn't like it? What if she did? What else would he want to do? Even as her rational mind hesitated, her body eagerly surrendered. Her pussy flooded with moisture, her womb clenched and her hips lifted, ready and receptive. Her chest tightened with a strange yearning, a yearning she sensed that only he could fulfill.

"Jamie?"

She bit her lip. "Yes…Reese."

"What?"

"Yes…sir, please spank me."

She was rewarded with an open palm to her left cheek. It stung fiercely, and she yelped. For some strange reason, she hadn't expected it to *hurt*. They were playing, for goodness sake. Then came the second slap, even harder than the first, on the other cheek. He paused, and she tensed, waiting for the next smack. She didn't know what she expected to feel, but this wasn't it. It wasn't erotic. It was just…painful. She'd entered into this willingly, eagerly, but doubts assailed her. Tears prickled her eyes as his hand burned her buttocks several more times. She was considering ordering him to stop when the next crack of his hand on her ass sent an electrifying current of pleasure reverberating through her body, to her clitoris, her cunt, her womb. She gasped, her eyes widening in surprise.

Another spank and her clit pulsed in delight, her pussy releasing a flood of moisture, and Jamie couldn't contain her moan of pleasure. There was still pain, yes, but what delicious pain it was. Wanton desire cascaded through her, ignited by the flames spiraling from her burning ass to her clit, her cunt, her clenching womb. Intense satisfaction flooded through her, as if the spanking awoke some deep latent need to be dominated, to revel in a man's expression of controlled power. Her mind couldn't make sense of the gratification that coursed through her, but she knew she'd never felt as alive, as sexy, as she did in this moment.

"Oh God, don't stop." When the next blow came, she raised her ass to receive it, savoring the scorching pleasure. He spanked her until rapture and pain became one, and she whimpered and pleaded for more in a high keening voice. She didn't recognize this woman crouched on all fours begging to be spanked by a man she'd just met. Where was the Jamie she knew?

"Yes, Jamie, that's it. You're a good girl." The rumble of his voice wrapped around her like a thick woolen blanket, kindling warmth deep within her chest. It thrilled her she had pleased him. Hands that had spanked, now caressed, soothing the sting but not the desire. "Your ass is blushing so pretty," he said. "Your cunt is dripping."

He penetrated her with two fingers, stroking in and out of her wet depths. He thrummed over her clit, tormenting the tiny bud until every nerve and muscle in her body craved release. She could feel her wetness running down her thighs and the bulleted points of her nipples hurt.

She shuddered as he pressed his lips to her burning ass cheeks, then trailed his tongue to her opening, licking her from clit to slit, searing her aching aroused flesh.

Jamie feared her body would burst into flames. She'd never felt such an overwhelming hunger, desire for a man, a specific man. "Oh God, Reese…please," she cried. She wanted his mouth on her, his fingers inside her. She craved the sharp smacks that made her pleasure so much more intense. "I need you, Reese, spank me, fuck me please…"

His palm seared her throbbing, inflamed ass cheeks, and a keening cry escaped her.

When he pressed his cock to her cunt, her body, well beyond ready, opened to receive him, and he surged inside, huge and hard. Satisfaction had her clenching around him. He felt as if he were made for her—as if they were two complimentary parts of a whole that had finally been united. As he thrust, his cock stroked her clit, setting it afire. She burned with hunger, a driving life force that propelled her own hips into motion, so that she met his thrusts with her own. Her clit pulsed in aching anticipation, and she felt her pussy tightening around his cock. She was scarcely aware of Reese lubing his fingers in her juices until he pressed against her puckered anus and penetrated her channel with a finger. Jamie cried out in alarm and protest, wanting to dislodge the foreign presence, but the invasive pressure felt so shamefully satisfying, her body overruled her sensibilities and began to rock.

Reese buried his finger inside her, reaming her. Her body was filled with his presence, and though her mind rebelled, her body eagerly accepted the raw, sharp pleasure that seared her clit, her pussy, her womb, her tender, previously inviolate anal channel. The tension in her clit and in her pussy swelled to a crescendo of sensation. Ecstasy rocketed through her and she drove against his finger, against his cock, and she tumbled into an abyss of painful rapture. Reese shouted as his cock throbbed, and he emptied himself inside her.

***

His, Reese thought with satisfaction as his ardor cooled and rational thought returned to him. He brushed his lips against the nape of her neck and her shoulders as his free hand lightly caressed the silky smooth skin of her breasts and stomach. His desire momentarily satisfied, he still wanted—needed—to touch her. Jamie Douglass, soon to be Jamie Nichols, was *his*. His gut had been correct as usual. She was the woman he wanted to spank and cuddle. Fuck and make love to. Discipline and spoil. She aroused his tenderness as much as his lust and dominance.

She was naturally submissive, hard-wired to surrender herself to her lover, though he doubted she realized it. Her surprised reaction revealed she'd never been spanked, but she'd yielded instinctively, first accepting, then encouraging his erotic discipline. She'd disrobed on command, learned quickly how to suck him by following his unspoken instruction, and obeyed all his verbal commands. But it had been the sweet way she'd raised her ass to receive her spanking that had rocked him to the core and convinced him she was naturally submissive.

Spanking Jamie had been a complete carnal sensory experience of sight, touch, sound, smell and taste. Seeing her on her hands and knees, awaiting his erotic discipline, had made his chest clench. Her creamy white ass had colored to a delicate pink. The sound of his palms stinging the softness of her cheeks had mingled with the sweet music of her breathy moans and pleas. The folds of her cunt had swelled, her pussy creaming, growing wetter with each erotic slap, releasing an aroma of hot, wet sex. He hadn't been able to resist tasting her. She'd tasted like heaven.

He had much more to show her, teach her. He envisioned long weekends when he would partake of the pleasures of her body at leisure. He wanted to eat her sweet cunt until she screamed, spank her until she couldn't sit down on anything but his throbbing cock, fuck her in every position recorded by the Kama Sutra, and ream her tight, receptive asshole as she begged for more.

Her virgin asshole. He was certain she'd never let anyone take her anally, and it thrilled him to know he would be the first. And the only.

Their bodies were still connected, and Jamie was wiggling now, trying to dislodge his embedded finger. That had been her only resistance, her only protest to his possession. Besides her cry of protest, he had felt her initial recoil. But her body had responded to his possession, craved it. Just as her pussy had convulsed around his cock, her anal muscles had contracted around his finger. She might require a little coaxing, but it was just a matter of time before Jamie surrendered herself totally to the most intimate possession.

Reese slowly released her. A sheen of moisture glistened on her soft skin; her cunt was swollen and wet, her buttocks tinted pink. She looked like a woman who'd been thoroughly and completely fucked. Except that he wasn't finished with her yet. He doubted he would ever be done.

He stretched out and pulled her into his arms, spoon-style. She made a contented sound, her rosy ass nestling in the cradle of his hips. She curved into him as if she were made for him, which she was.

"Sweet girl," he murmured.

His hands cupped her beautiful, sexy breasts. She had most incredible nipples, large, responsive. Reese was pleased to discover she liked a firm touch, liked it when he tugged and twisted. He pinched one now and was rewarded with the tightening of the bud and a muffled sound of pleasure. He loved the moans and cries she made. He couldn't wait to see how she reacted when he attached nipple clamps to her gorgeous tits. He was also eager to see her pussy waxed and bare for him. But first things first. He had to marry her so she understood once and for all time that she was his.

***

This was insane! *She* was insane. Jamie's head spun in dismay. Reese had taken possession of not just her body, but her heart as well. She feared she'd fallen in love with him. What was wrong with her? She wasn't the type to fall in love at first sight! She didn't fuck men she'd just met! As much as that rocked her foundation, what scared her most was realizing she yearned to give this man whatever he asked for. He could ask her to crawl over hot coals, and she would do it to please him.

She couldn't exist just to love another person, to serve his needs. She was raised to be independent, self-sufficient, to stand on her own two feet. It shamed her that it felt so right, so perfect, to bow on her hands and knees and be spanked, that it made her feel complete as a woman to await and obey his commands.

Heat crept into her face as she thought of the things she'd done, the way she'd presented herself like a bitch in heat, letting—no begging—him to spank her, to fuck her, the way she'd moaned and cried out in ecstasy. She wasn't a moaner, a screamer, she wasn't! Oh God, she'd even let him stick his finger up her ass. She should have made him stop, but instead she'd rocked against him, craving that depraved penetration. It had propelled her into the most intense orgasm she'd ever had.

Never had she experienced such a loss of self-control, a desperate desire to surrender everything she thought she was. She was going to have to be more resolute in the future. She couldn't deny the bond between her and Reese, but she *could* maintain what little sense of self she still possessed. She had to. For her own self-worth she couldn't give him everything. She needed to keep something of herself for herself.

Even now, after a mind-blowing orgasm that should have sated her, her body wanted more. Her nipples were beading as he stroked them. Her pussy was clenching in response to his growing cock, nestled snugly between her ass cheeks, still tender from the spanking. Unlike her previous lovers, he didn't fumble around. He seemed to know unerringly what she liked, and her body responded automatically to his mastery. He was the virtuoso violinist, and she, his instrument.

"You are so perfect, Jamie," Reese's voice rumbled in her ear. "You were made for me."

"Yes," she agreed, and shifted to allow him access as his fingers dipped between her thighs and found her clit. He stroked the little bud and her breath caught in her throat.

"I think we can get two seats on a flight to Las Vegas tonight," he said.

"Vegas?" she gasped. "Why?"

"So we can get married."

***

One year later

Jamie was winding her way through the crowded room in search of Reese when someone grabbed her elbow.

"Jamie! It is you. Someone said you were here, but I didn't believe it."

Jamie turned to see Elisa Castile, a friend she hadn't seen in months. "Of course it's me. Why wouldn't you believe it?" She hugged Elisa tightly. "It's so good to see you."

"You've kept quite a low profile since you *eloped* last year," Elisa said.

Jamie flushed. It was still a sore spot with some of her friends that they hadn't been invited to the marriage ceremony in Las Vegas. She tried to explain that she would have invited them to the wedding if she had known there was going to be one. But it was probably best that they weren't there. They would have been shocked to hear independent, career-minded Jamie Douglass vow to love, honor and *obey*.

"I know. I'm sorry. I have no excuse, but Reese has been traveling a lot and I've been going with him."

"You're not back to work then?" Elisa peered at her.

"No. I'm officially a domestic goddess," she joked. People

were always asking her about that. In some private, less-than-polite circles, she'd been called everything from a trophy wife to a gold digger. She shrugged it off. She loved being her husband's wife and partner, making a home for him. They didn't understand how much of her time was taken up by managing a large house, traveling and doing assorted wifely tasks and errands. She wanted to be relaxed and welcoming when Reese arrived home, not frenzied and stressed.

"Ah. He didn't want you to work." Elisa nodded knowingly.

"Reese wouldn't have a problem with my having a career, but I decided it would be best for both of us, if I didn't work outside the home," Jamie corrected her.

"Well, you obviously made the right choice because you look wonderful. You're practically glowing, and that dress you have on is gorgeous." Elisa eyed the simple ivory silk shift that flowed over Jamie's curves.

"Thank you. I think the 'glow' is a holdover from the tan I got in the Caribbean. We just returned from a two-week vacation," Jamie explained, omitting to mention that said tan was an all-over one because she and Reese had frolicked on a private beach where clothing was most definitely optional.

Elisa leaned in close. "I think you look so good because you're getting lots of mind-blowing sex."

"She is." Reese materialized beside her.

Elisa giggled as Jamie blushed.

Reese curved his arm around Jamie's waist. "Here's your champagne." He handed her a glass of sparkling wine. "Sorry I was gone so long; there was a line at the bar, and then Ralph cornered me and wanted to talk business. I broke away as soon as I could."

"You can't ignore a client when you're attending a party at his house," Jamie said.

"I should have been more considerate of you," he said.

"Reese, you remember Elisa, don't you? You met a few months ago at another party."

"Certainly. How are you, Elisa?"

"Great, thank you." She shook his hand. "If you'll excuse me, I'd better go find my other half. I haven't seen him since we got here. Don't be a stranger, Jamie."

"I won't. We should do lunch."

"I'd love to. Call me." Elisa hugged Jamie.

"I will," Jamie said.

Elisa disappeared into the crowd.

"She's right you know. You do glow." His eyes were warm as he looked at her.

Jamie shook her head. "I'm just happy." She was. Everything in her life was perfect.

Well, almost.

There was that one little thing. If the large and growing elephant in their marriage could be called little.

She had promised to obey, to submit to her husband's authority, and it wasn't a vow she'd made lightly. He cherished and disciplined her, in bed and out. Through their marriage, she had come to recognize submissiveness as her true nature and had blossomed under Reese's mastery. If, on occasion, she challenged his authority, it was because the punishment for disobedience was so exquisite. She often suspected that her husband loved her gestures of defiance for the same reason.

But, she couldn't—wouldn't—allow him to penetrate her anally. He had fucked her in every other way possible, but somehow that one act seemed too intimate. It meant her total surrender and once she did that, she would have nothing left of herself, nothing left to give. Her steadfast refusal was becoming an issue.

"Are you ready to leave?" Reese was asking now.

She looked up at him. "Whenever you are."

"Let's go. I'm in need of my wife." His heated look left no doubt about what he needed, and flickers of desire licked at her nerve endings. Even after a year of marriage, it amazed her how quickly he aroused her, with a simple touch, a look, or a whisper. His voice could turn her on with a recitation of the IRS tax code. Hearing his sexual commands spoken in his gravelly voice ignited her libido instantly.

"What are you grinning about?" Reese asked.

"You." Jamie smiled broader. "I was thinking how sexy you are, and how lucky I am."

Reese's dark gaze swept over her from head to toe, leaving Jamie feeling as if she'd been stripped naked. Of course, she very nearly was. The ivory slip of a dress that Elisa had so admired was the only thing she had on except for her gold high-heeled sandals and a simple diamond pendant. In deference to Reese's wishes, she wore no bra, no panties. He liked to know she was completely accessible to him.

"I bought you a present," he said.

Her fingers curled around her necklace, a gift he'd given her that morning. "Another one?" she protested. "Reese, you're spoiling me."

Her husband frequently surprised her with gifts from small to extravagant: a love letter, a single rose, a new book by her favorite author, minuscule scraps of lingerie or jewelry. And sex toys. Her nightstand contained a veritable treasure trove of items he used to bring her to shuddering gratification.

"You're my wife. It's my right to spoil you if I choose," he said possessively. Then his voice lowered. "Besides, this one isn't for public show."

"Oh." Her lips parted and her pussy convulsed, gushing wet heat even as uneasiness skittered along her spine. Lately, most of his sex toys were related to anal stimulation: slim vibrators, smooth beads, supple dildos and butt plugs. She knew his intention was to show her how pleasurable anal play could be, to lead her toward the ultimate completion.

She submitted shamefully, lustfully to the former, but drew the line at absolute possession.

She knew the clock ticked on his patience. Each new anal sex toy he used on her brought them one step closer to a showdown that made Jamie afraid she'd be forced to make a heart-wrenching choice between hanging onto herself or her marriage.

Reese's grasped her hip, guiding her through the crowd. They said goodbye to their host and went outside. Their car retrieved by valet, Reese assisted her into it and shut the door. He was so solicitous in that way and in many others. He often cooked for her and always helped her with the dishes. Evenings, they'd sit together in front of the TV while he massaged her feet. At those times, his innate dominance receded. But in bed, it returned in full force. There Reese smoothly, deliberately, firmly controlled the action of their lovemaking and her responses.

Reese waved at the guard as he drove through the entrance of their gated community and pulled into their circular driveway, parking beneath the portico of their house. "House" was actually too insignificant a word to describe the grand structure, filled as it was with marble, crystal, exotic wood and imported European antique furnishings. When they married, Reese had sold his penthouse in the city and had purchased this home for Jamie. Her friends referred to it as the Taj Mahal.

Reese exited the vehicle and helped Jamie out of the car. The warm summer night whispered over her skin as they walked hand-in-hand to the door. Under her dress, the faint summer breeze teased her moist naked pussy, truly bare since she now waxed.

Her heels clicked loudly on the marbled floor of the rotunda as they made their way to the staircase. Side by side they climbed the winding stair, Jamie clutching the gilded banister for support. Once in their master suite, Jamie moved to the bedside, and watching her husband, awaited his cue.

Reese approached her, and ran a finger down the side of her face to her lips. Her mouth parted as he traced her lips, her skin burning where he touched her. "You look amazing," Reese said. "All I could think of tonight is how much I wanted to do this." His hands slid down her shoulders and released the thin straps, allowing her dress to slide off her body. She kicked off her gilded mule sandals and stepped out of the pool of silk.

She unbuttoned his shirt and he shrugged it off. She

unzipped his pants, allowing her fingers to brush his cock, then tugged the pants down his lean hips. His underwear hooked on his erection, but she freed it and released his hard, throbbing manhood. The glistening head was too much to resist, and she captured it in her mouth, her tongue hungrily lapping at the pearly essence she found.

Reese sucked in a harsh gasp of air. Jamie sucked hard, transferring all of her lust, and a vague yearning she couldn't put a name to, into pleasuring her husband. She worked voraciously, her head bobbing, her breasts swinging.

He was getting close to coming when he stopped her. Jamie straightened and stared at him. The air weighed heavy with tension. The muscles of his face were corded and taut, his eyes were lit with lust and a savage determination—and so fleeting she thought it must be a trick of the light—regret.

She shivered, craving desperately, painfully to have him touch her in a way she would never forget, to feel marked by him.

His eyes glittered. "Let me give you your present." He extracted a wrapped box from his nightstand drawer.

Jamie held her breath as she undid the paper, her tension easing when she saw a velvet jeweler's box. She pried open the lid and found an intricately looped gold chain with several golden balls attached.

"Is it a necklace?"

"It's a nipple chain," he answered. "It's eighteen karat gold. I explained to the jeweler what I wanted and he crafted it for me."

She drew it out of the box, now noticing the tension-sprung rings, and the weightiness that belied its delicacy. It was several chains really. One long one to tether her breasts together, and six short strands, three of which would dangle from each banded nipple. At the end of each short strand was a solid gold pea-sized sphere.

"It's lovely," she said.

"You're lovely." He took the empty box from her and tossed

it aside. His head bent and he seized her left nipple in his mouth. Jamie moaned as he tormented the bud to a tight pebble. She clutched the chain in one hand, while the other wound itself in his thick hair.

His mouth released her nipple, his fingers further pinching and tugging the bud, and then captured the other between his lips and teeth. When both nipples were elongated, turgid, aching points, he took the chain from her, adjusted the tension on the bands, and deftly clamped a ring tightly around each nipple.

Jamie gasped at searing, delicious pain. Blood coursed through her ears as her heart thumped. Her head reeled.

"I made it tighter than what you're used to. Can you take it?" Reese asked.

Jamie nodded. The biting pain was warming to a blissful ache.

"I want you to burn for me, Jamie. Go get a butt plug."

Her pussy let down more moisture, and her anal sphincter spasmed in anticipation. "Reese..." Her knees quivered. She shook her head as the war between resistance and eager obedience raged within her. Anal play always elicited this reaction in her—her mind whispering for her to resist, her body shouting for her to surrender.

"Do it, Jamie," he ordered. "Get the new one. The large one."

Jamie swallowed hard. On quaking legs, she moved to her nightstand. With each step, the weighted balls tugged on her burning nipples, transmitting fiery sensations throughout her body. She extracted the huge but flexible tapered sex toy and a tube of anal cream.

Knowing what he expected, she lubed the plug and then handed it to him. Spreading her legs, she bent over. She flinched as the cold wetness touched her back entrance. The ring of muscles guarding her anal channel gave only slight resistance before relaxing to allow the invading object in. Her rectum clutched the plug greedily, and Jamie stifled a moan of shameful pleasure. The toy felt huge inside her, pressing against sensitive tissues, igniting a familiar craving for more.

Reese reclined on the bed. "Sit on me. Let me eat your pussy."

It was a command she was more than willing to obey. Her stomach clenched in anticipation, desire whipping through her. She reveled in the intimacy and devotion of oral sex. It made her feel loved, indulged.

Jamie straddled his head, positioning herself over his mouth. Growling, he rubbed his face over her vulva. Jamie inhaled sharply as his rough beard grazed her aroused, swollen flesh. His breath caressed her, and she felt herself dissolving into a pool of molten desire. She needed this contact with him, craved it.

"Ah, Jamie. You smell wet and hot—like life itself." Tingles of pleasure skipped over her at his adoring words and lust-laden tone.

He worshipped her with his touch, his tongue touching her delicately, circling the protective hood of her clit, coaxing her to greater desire. Her body hummed with arousal, her head reeling as if she were intoxicated. He drew her inner labia into his mouth and suckled gently before peeling back her folds with his fingers and exposing her to his marauding mouth. She sucked in her breath as her clit throbbed. Her body was strung as tight as piano wire. His tongue trailed down to her opening where he lapped her cream. His throat rumbled with satisfaction. Then he returned to her clit, lashing and suckling on the sensitive bud. She needed more, needed it fast. A driving, primal urge took command of her body, forcing her hips to rock against his mouth. The motion caused the weighted clamps to yank sharply. Painful pleasure ricocheted between her inflamed clit and her shackled cherried nipples. Each tug on her nipples made her hips move faster; each sway of her body electrified the sensitive tips of her breasts with a savage fire.

Reese grasped the flared base of the plug and began to pump it in her ass, increasing the deliciously shameful pleasure, driving it deep. Her very being was consumed by the carnality of his possession. She felt hot and cold at the same time, her body wracked by fever and chills simultaneously.

Jamie was powerless before the sensations that Reese commanded from her. Her rectum contracted, and she whimpered in delight and protest, buffeted on a wave of raw rapture. She didn't want to enjoy it, didn't want her body to rock between his relentless flicking tongue and the anal toy.

Her emotions seesawed. She was being torn apart by the savage ecstasy rocketing through her—her sex was on fire, but so was her ass.

Reese's fingers replaced his mouth, moving fast and hard over her clit, stroking her toward climax. "Do you see how it could be, Jamie? It could be me inside you, me filling your sweet ass, fucking you. Let me take you, Jamie. Now."

"No." She choked, her hips moving frantically. Why did it have to come to this? Why did he have to force her to choose? She didn't want to have to deny him. Didn't want to keep denying herself, fighting against the secret, seductive whispers deep inside that urged her to submit.

She was perched at the edge of a precipice, and some inner voice was compelling her to jump, to abandon herself in the ultimate, wanton surrender. She wanted it so badly her heart hurt as if in the grip of a vise. She ached with the need to take that leap, to submit utterly and completely to her husband, but her mind held her fast. There would be nothing left of her, for her, if she relinquished the vestiges of her control.

"Then take me," he bit out.

She cried out in protest and distress as he ceased stroking, but then sighed in satisfaction as his strong arms shifted her over his hips. Gratefully, she sank onto his hard cock, forcing it deep inside her slick pussy, ignoring the burn as delicate tissues struggled to accommodate double penetration. There was no space inside her, only a driving pressure, not only in her ass and cunt, but also in her heart.

Frantically, she rode his cock, impaling herself on him

over and over. His thick shaft tore into her, catching her clit with every upstroke and downstroke, robbing her of every sane, rational thought except easing the relentless ache. Reese met her thrusts with his own; their bodies slammed together in tandem. The gold weights swung madly, pulling on her engorged, distended nipples, the piercing pleasure urging her to move faster, harder.

The tension mounted, searing, agonizing. "I'm going to come. Oh God, Reese," she cried out.

"Yes, Jamie. Now," he growled and released the clamps.

A burst of fire shot through her nipples, rocketing her into orgasm. Jamie screamed as her body exploded, involuntary contractions undulating through her clit, her cunt, her womb and her rectum. Reese uttered a hoarse cry as he came forcefully.

Jamie slumped on top of her husband. His hands smoothed over her back, gently stroking. A few moments later, he rolled her off him, removed the plug and strode into the bathroom. She heard water running. When he emerged, with a towel wrapped around his waist, he held a wet cloth. He cleaned between her legs and her cheeks. He disposed of the cloth in the bathroom and then came and stood by the bed.

***

Reese regarded his wife steadily. She lay curled in the rumpled bed sheets, exhausted. Her response to him had been passionate, lustful, fiery.

And inhibited, uncommitted, elusive.

As he'd made love to her, he had sensed the ambivalence churning within her, had been able to feel her reluctance to abandon herself totally to the pleasure she was capable of, that he could give her.

He'd felt her longing, her anguish. She didn't know it, but it was evident in her yearning glances, her sad expressions, her impassioned, but almost desperate responses to his intimate caresses. It was as if she were trying to fill a primal hunger with everything but the one thing that would truly satisfy it.

Reese didn't care about anal sex. Sure, he enjoyed it. Wanted it with his wife. But it wasn't the act itself, but what it represented that made it so important. He needed to know that his wife loved him enough to give him everything, he needed to know that she held nothing back. He needed her complete trust and total surrender.

As he needed it, so did she. She needed it more, in fact. His sweet, sexy wife was made to submit, to surrender to her mate. She was denying an essential, basic part of her sexuality, and would never feel complete until she acknowledged it. Lived it. And if she didn't find her true self with him, eventually Reese feared she would start looking elsewhere and he would lose her. She brought the light to his day, the warmth to his night. Without her, all he'd achieved in his life would be worthless.

She was hurting. Because she hurt, he hurt. He wanted to slam his fist in the wall with frustration. Why couldn't she see what was in front of her? Patiently, for the past year he'd tried to coax her toward ultimate completion, to no avail.

It was like entering a swimming pool. Some people dived in, abandoning themselves to the pleasures of the water, while others held back, attempting to wade in, inch by chilling inch.

If Jamie didn't take the plunge soon, she would be stuck in the shallow end, true gratification out of reach. He couldn't make her take the plunge. He could only take it himself.

Looking down at his wife, Reese made his decision. He took a deep breath. "Our one-year anniversary is in two weeks," he said. They had reservations at a bed and breakfast along the coast.

She nodded, a questioning look on her face. A muscle began to twitch in his jaw, but he steeled his courage. "I'm not going to touch you again until then."

Jamie sprang upright, but before she could form a sentence, he spoke. "Between now and our anniversary, you need to decide if you're going to submit to me or not. If you don't decide, I will."

Tears filled her eyes. "You're saying if we don't have anal sex, then we're—"

"This isn't about sex, Jamie." Reese said quietly. "But even if it was, I'm not asking you to do something you don't want to do. This is about trust. This is about you withholding your soul from me. You're not being honest about your needs. Your heart and your body want to submit to me. You need it and I need it. I want all of you, not just part of you. You've made being fucked in the ass some sort of line in the sand. It's an arbitrary barrier, and until it's down, you'll never be truly fulfilled, never truly happy with yourself. If you're not happy with yourself, you won't be happy with me.

"I am happy!" she cried.

He shrugged. "You think you are. And for now, maybe," he conceded. "But for how long?"

"Reese, don't do this, please. I love you!"

The pain in her voice squeezed his heart. It almost made him relent, but he forced himself to stick to his decision. "I love you, too. That's why I have to do this. I should have dealt with this sooner, but I thought if I gave you time, you'd come around. It's all or nothing, Jamie. I'm sorry, but that's the way it has to be." He paused. "I'll sleep in one of the guest rooms tonight."

Without another glance, he strode out of the room and shut the door.

***

Reese's heart clenched as he listened to Jamie's sobbing through the closed bedroom door. Her cries knifed through him, tearing him up inside. He couldn't stand to hear her cry any time—knowing that he was the cause of her tears made it ten times worse. It nearly weakened his resolve. He had nothing to go on but his own gut instinct that he was right to force the issue. He'd made risky decisions before, but those involved cut-and-dried business matters, not his wife, the woman he loved. If this didn't work out and he lost her…no, he wouldn't even consider that. Failure was not an option. This was the only way to ensure their future happiness. He stalked down the hallway to the guest wing and went into the first room he came to.

As he'd told her, if this had just been about anal sex, he would not have forced the issue. If she found it distasteful or his size hurt her, he would have accepted her refusal. But that wasn't the case. Her sweet puckered asshole was eager to be penetrated, opened to accommodate any toy he chose to use, clutching at it greedily, hungrily. It never failed to push her over the edge of orgasmic bliss. And today, he'd used a plug that was nearly as large around as he was. She could take him. She just wouldn't. It was as if she were jealously guarding one secret part of herself.

That hurt. His sweet and fiery wife was hard-wired for obedience and submission and the pleasure only he could bring her. Her sexual nature required utter surrender to be complete. As his required mastery and authority.

Jamie was his soul's mate. He, dominant; she, submissive— two parts that completed a whole. Uncomplicated, yet incendiary when the two parts united. Submitting to him would free her, awaken her to her soul's secret desire, bring her deepest yearnings out of the dark into the light where he could nurture them.

If she submitted to him, she would blossom in ways she had yet to imagine. Her body knew what her soul craved. Yet her mind resisted.

He could sense that she felt shamed by her needs. Only by facing her needs, indulging them, luxuriating in them, would she free herself from that dark cloud. He needed to help her indulge her desires, to luxuriate in them.

***

Two weeks later

Jamie slumped at her bedroom dressing table listening to the water run as Reese showered in the bathroom. She wore only a wispy thong, heels and a satin robe. She needed to finish dressing, but had no energy for it. *Happy anniversary to me.* Unhappy anniversary was more like it. How quickly her marriage had changed.

Reese had returned to sleeping in their bed after the first night that he spent in the guest room, but he had held fast to his promise not to touch her. Instead, they tiptoed around each other like two overly polite strangers, their conversations limited to comments about the weather and requests to pass the salt.

Nighttimes were the worst. Jamie would clutch the edge of the bed, curled into a ball of hurt and sexual arousal as Reese turned his back to her, shutting her out. She could tell from his breathing he wasn't sleeping. Sleep eluded her, too. She couldn't sleep when her heart was breaking.

She had to give him a decision.

The problem was she didn't know what it would be. She had no idea what she was going to tell him.

It wasn't right for him to force her to make a choice like this.

And it wasn't right that despite his ultimatum, she wanted him so much she ached.

She spent every conscious moment wracked by sexual arousal. Her body was on fire; she couldn't think, couldn't concentrate, and couldn't focus beyond the gnawing sexual tension. Her breasts were heavy and full; her nipples, in a state of perpetual hardness, hurt. Her vulva was swollen and engorged, her pussy creaming.

Since they'd met, they'd never gone a day without making love. She tried taking care of her roiling sexual need herself, but it didn't relieve the physical ache, or the yearning in her heart.

Only Reese could do that. She craved the connection of mind, body, and soul that could only be expressed by joining with his body, submitting to him, drawing on his power and strength. He wanted that contact, too. She could see it in his clenched jaw, his tense posture, the erection he couldn't hide. Yet, he continued to deny her the very thing he wanted to give her.

Like she had denied him. Isn't that what Reese meant?

She rebelled at the thought. Yes, he was the head of their household, and it was her duty to obey, but it wasn't fair that he had ordered to her choose.

The shower shut off, and she could hear Reese moving about the bathroom. She couldn't force him to relent; that would never work. He was one hundred percent pure dominance, fully in charge, fully in control. He desired her, yes, but his iron will kept his voracious libido contained. She'd never been able to push him to the brink of his self-control the way he did her.

But had she ever tried? Maybe her assumptions were wrong. Jamie stared at herself in the mirror as an idea hatched in her mind. Quickly she brushed out her hair and rose to her feet. Before she lost her courage, she let her robe fall to the floor.

Faking an assurance she didn't feel, Jamie glided into the bathroom. Reese, dressed in a pair of slacks, sans shirt, was shaving at his sink. He glanced at her in the mirror, and froze. A muscle twitched in his cheek, but he continued shaving as if she weren't there.

She moved to her vanity and pulled open a drawer, bending over to search inside, presenting her near-naked backside toward Reese. "Hmm," she mused. "I thought it was in here." She rummaged around a little more.

"Have you seen my gold hair clip?" she improvised. She didn't own a gold hair clip.

"No." He wasn't looking at her, but a vein throbbed in his temple.

She straightened and moved closer to him so that the turgid tips of her breasts brushed his arm. He flinched and nicked himself with the razor.

"Are you sure?" She peered at him innocently. "It's one of

those claw kinds. Has rhinestones on it?"

"No." His jaw tightened. "Could you give me some space, please? I'm trying to shave."

"You missed a spot." She touched his cheek, then trailed her finger over his jaw, his neck, and down to his hard, muscled chest. She touched his flat male nipple and it hardened instantly. He'd look so sexy with a piercing, she thought.

Scowling, Reese grabbed her hand and thrust it away. "You know the rules, Jamie."

She shrugged, watching as his gaze was drawn to her naked breasts. She needed him to suck on her nipples so bad. Needed to feel his hands on her, his fingers inside her, his cock filling her. "I didn't make those rules," she protested.

"No, I made the rules. And you'd do well to obey them." He faced her now, arrogance etched in every taut muscle.

She arched her eyebrows. "Or?"

"Or you'll experience the consequences." He tossed aside the razor and wiped the traces of shaving cream from his face with a towel.

Jamie moved behind him and pressed her breasts to his back, rubbing her hard, aching nipples against his smooth, heated skin. Her palms flattened on his muscled abdomen, then strayed lower. His cock, fully erect, leapt at her touch. A secret feminine thrill raced through her. There were some things her husband couldn't control. "Promises, promises," she purred.

Jamie squealed as Reese snapped. He whipped around, breaking her hold. Grabbing her wrist, he dragged her into the bedroom, hauling her to a settee where he yanked her over his lap. She wiggled, trying to get away, but he was too strong for her.

She heard the rip of fabric as he tore off her panties. His palm came down hard on her ass, and Jamie cried out.

He rained burning slaps on her bare bottom, faster and harder than he'd ever spanked her before, and Jamie realized the spanking wasn't intended as erotic loveplay, but was meant for serious discipline. Too bad her traitorous swollen pussy didn't know the difference. She was creaming, her juices running down her thighs.

"You think this is a game?" He spanked her several times, hard sharp slaps.

Humiliated that she was being punished, that it sent lust careening through her body, her eyes filled with tears.

"Answer me!" He growled, spanking her several more times.

"No," she choked. Her ass was on fire. She probably wouldn't be able to sit down for a week, but each smack sent excruciating pleasure ricocheting through her clit, her cunt, her womb. He was not unmoved either. His cock was rock hard and throbbing, digging into her abdomen.

"No, what?" He burned her right cheek with an especially sharp spank. Her vagina contracted, and she bit back a moan.

"No, sir," she muttered, mutiny in her voice.

"What was that?" Two stinging slaps kissed her ass.

"No, sir!" she repeated louder, but omitted the sarcasm.

He struck her again. "I told you the next time…" His words were punctuated by two hard, sharp spanks. …"I fucked you it would be to fuck your tight little ass. Submit to me, Jamie." After weeks of not touching her at all, his forceful discipline ignited a raging desire that overran her senses like an out-of-control locomotive. Her body was engulfed by flames, and she could do little to douse the fire.

Jamie whimpered as Reese pressed a finger slickened with her juices against her puckered asshole. She willed her body to resist, but it surrendered eagerly. The tight brown ring relaxed, and his finger slid in easily. He added a second and third, stretching her tight back entrance with delicious pressure.

She moaned, lifting her bottom to thrust against his impaling fingers, urging him deeper, harder, faster.

And then his fingers were gone. He stung her ass cheeks five more times and released her. She rolled to the floor, wincing as she landed on her tender bottom.

"I'm going to the office," he stated, towering over her.

Work? She stared at him. He was going to work? It was their anniversary!

"I'll expect you to meet me there in an hour with your answer."

***

Reese slammed his fist on his mahogany desk. What the hell was he thinking?

Don't look back had always been his motto. He ruled his life and business by doing what needed to be done and accepting the consequences. Take no prisoners, feel no fear.

He was scared now, the knot in his chest telling him he'd made the biggest mistake of his life. No, not one. Several. And each one compounded the egregiousness of the previous one.

Whatever had possessed him to force Jamie to choose between all or nothing? It wasn't as if she expected him to be satisfied with a few crumbs of affection she tossed his way. She'd given him almost the entire loaf, damn *near* everything she had. And he, idiot that he was, had insisted on the crumbs, too. Why?

Reese sucked in a hard breath. What if she didn't show this morning? All or nothing. What if she showed up and chose nothing? Told him to take a flying leap? What then?

His gut had insisted his wife was ready to surrender completely, but what did Jamie's gut tell her? Get lost, loser? Christ on a broomstick. Reese raked a hand through his thick hair.

So that had been his first mistake. His second had been subjecting them both to two weeks of abstinence. But he hadn't stopped at withholding sex; he'd withheld his love as well. He'd lain in bed night after night, gritting his teeth, making no move to hold her, listening to her muffle her sobs as she cried herself to sleep. Even though he'd acted like a bastard, she still wanted him. He could smell her need for him in the sweet, musky scent of her creaming pussy, see it in the pointed peaks of her breasts, the beseeching look in her eyes.

It made him want her even more until his own need clawed at his skin. He'd been unable to concentrate on anything except the memory of her wet slick depths, her pebbled sensitive nipples, her soft skin, and her breathless pleas for release. His balls ached. His cock grew so hard he feared the skin would burst.

Yeah, he showed her, all right. Showed her what a fucking moron he was.

And then this morning, their anniversary—wasn't that perfect?—he'd topped it all off by losing control. She'd defied him, attempted to seduce him, and he'd snapped. He'd intended to punish her, paddle her for her disobedience, but she'd turned that around with her sweet submission, her breathless arousal.

Not since he was a teenager had he nearly come in his pants.

The way she unconsciously lifted her hips to receive each slap, the growing blush of her sweetly curved ass, the creaming of her pussy dampening the leg of his slacks had pushed him to the brink of his restraint. He'd almost fucked her then, taken her as he'd told her he wouldn't.

Oh, yeah. He'd showed her.

Like an ass, he'd lectured Jamie on facing the consequences of her actions, and now he faced the consequences of his. Karma was a bitch, he thought.

Reese pushed back from his desk and went to stare out the window. His heart began to thud as he spotted Jamie's little gold sports car zip into the parking lot.

* * *

Jamie hesitated outside her husband's office. She ran her hands down her hips, smoothing out imaginary wrinkles in her short black Armani pencil skirt. She patted her hair, tucked neatly into a French knot. She remembered the first time she stood in this spot quaking in her stilettos. This was worse.

The fact that the sexual need that had dogged her for

two weeks had been intensified this morning didn't help her edginess. Every step caused the smooth silk of her ivory lace blouse to brush against her painfully hard nipples and heightened her awareness of her swollen, weeping pussy.

"It's now or never," she muttered and entered the office.

The receptionist's desk was vacant, as she knew it would be since it was Saturday. The door to her husband's private suite was closed, and Jamie played with a manicured fingernail. Should she knock? Or wait?

She was saved from deciding when the door was flung open.

"You're here." Some intense emotion flashed across Reese's face before he masked it. His jaw was clenched, his eyes dark, unreadable. She'd hoped to see a softening, but there was none.

"You told me to be," she answered smoothly.

He muttered something she couldn't hear, but it sounded like 'moron.'

She frowned. "What?"

"Nothing." He shook his head. "Come in."

He stepped aside to let her pass. The door behind her clicked shut, and Jamie jumped, the hairs on the nape of her neck tingling, her stomach fluttering. She felt like a gazelle entering the lion's den. Her gaze darted around the opulent room, seeing but not appreciating the rich wood, the hand-tooled leather, the original artwork. She'd seen it all before, and it faded away before the decision she was facing.

"Jamie, look at me." Reese's tone was harsh.

She flinched.

He swore.

His large hands took hold of her upper arms, and she bit her lip, remembering the feel of those hands spanking her. Her stomach flip-flopped and her pussy clenched. Her breathing quickened. The air in the room grew hot, pressed heavily upon her as she lifted her gaze to the dark eyes of her husband.

She'd rehearsed a small speech, but the words evaporated.

"Would you like to sit down?"

She nodded. Her legs felt like jelly.

He led her to a chair fronting his desk, and Jamie lowered herself onto the hard wooden seat. She winced as her inflamed, aching buttocks protested.

He moved behind his desk and sank into his chair. "I'm sorry," he said. "I should not have spanked you that way."

Jamie wet her lips. "No. You were right," she said in a low voice.

He swallowed. "Can we start over?"

Jamie clutched her Kate Spade bag. "No."

Reese jerked. His hands clenched into fists. His mask of control shattered. She saw the naked pain in his eyes and realized how much he had been hurting.

"No," Jamie repeated, shaking her head. "We can't start over. But we can move forward...I'm ready, Reese."

"You don't have to do this." He glanced away, then back at her.

"I want to. I'm yours, Reese—heart, mind, soul and body. In any way you'll have me."

Reese's eyes blazed with a storm of emotions. "Let's go home, then."

Jamie shook her head. "No."

He grabbed for his telephone. "I'll call the inn and get us an early check-in."

"No. Now. Here." She rose to her feet and undid the clip that held her hair in place. She shook it loose. She gestured at the smooth, gleaming piece of furniture that stood between her and her husband. "I've always fantasized about you taking me on top of your desk," she said, unbuttoning her blouse.

She shrugged out of it, baring her breasts.

Reese inhaled sharply. "You're wearing the nipple chain."

Jamie's breasts, swollen with need, were heavy, the twin peaks pinched by the clamps to turgid ripeness like two cherries. She cupped her breasts and ran her thumbs over her engorged, hypersensitive nipples. "I put it on…" She peered at him through her lashes. "It's up to you to take it off." She paused. "But that's not all I'm wearing."

Savoring the avid, helpless lust etched on his face, she unzipped her skirt and tugged it down, revealing her smooth, waxed naked mound. Her clit throbbed, sending curls of lust skittering through her womb. She could smell her own pussy, wet, hot and musky.

"Come here, Jamie," he said thickly.

She smiled coquettishly. "Don't you want to see what else I'm wearing?" She turned and bent at the waist. Using her hands, she spread her ass cheeks to reveal an anal plug nestled in her cavity. She heard his sharp intake of breath.

"Come, here now," he growled when she faced him again. She extracted a tube of lubricant from her handbag. She'd made her decision, but nervousness at the import of it had her trembling as she rounded his desk. He pushed back on his chair and she slipped into the space provided, setting the lube on the desk.

His hands gently, reverently almost, cupped her breasts and he took one rigid, banded peak into his mouth. She flinched at the raw pleasure.

"Did I hurt you?" He looked at her.

"No." She moaned. "It feels good. Too good."

He removed the clamps, and blood surged into her nipples. She whimpered.

"Are you sure you want this, Jamie?" As he looked at her, the emotions he was feeling played out across his face: love, uncertainty, remorse, and desire. He would always be dominant, disciplining her when he saw the need, but his discipline would always be guided by love.

All vestiges of fear crumbled. Nothing mattered anymore except this, this moment, this man, this time. Her voice was strong as she spoke: "Yes, sir."

A triumphant growl erupted from his throat. He fastened onto her nipple, his gentle suction soothing and tormenting the hypersensitive bud. Her clit pulsed.

"Please…please…" Her hands clutched his muscled shoulders.

"Ssh, sweetheart. It's okay," he crooned. He shifted, sucking gently on her nipple's twin, then eased her onto his desk. She barely noticed the coolness, felt only the hard sleekness of smooth polished wood. She fell back onto her elbows and allowed him to spread her legs wide, baring her to his gaze—and anything else he might do.

Reese lowered his head. His warm breath caressed her aching flesh as his fingers parted her folds, opening her. His mouth came down on her sex, and she moaned in bliss. She'd needed this so much. Lived for it. He probed her cream-filled slit, and her hips came off the desk. His touch transported her to another world where nothing existed but the two of them and the ecstasy they would create together. Over and over he licked her, his faint beard rasping her flesh, his tongue teasing, then lashing, delving into her honeyed hole for its cream. He devoured her, revealing his own aching hunger, and her heart swelled with gratification. She wanted to be the one to fill his needs.

She heard him growl, "Just a little more, sweetheart, a little more," and licked and nibbled her everywhere, everywhere except where she needed it most—her clit. The hypersensitive flesh between her legs ached with heavenly tension too long denied. She needed him desperately in every possible way and needed him now. She shifted on the desk, raised her hips to maneuver him to the aching organ, but he resisted, teasing. Her fingers curled into his thick hair to tug his head upwards.

He leapt to his feet, and the chair careened into the paneled wall. He ripped off his shirt, then kicked off his shoes and socks, before tearing at the zipper of his pants. Trousers and shorts went flying. His massive rock-hard cock jutted out from his body, the huge knob purple and glistening with pre-come. He pulled her into his arms and kissed her, his mouth crushing her, his tongue plundering her. She could taste his need and her own on his lips. Jamie's hand wrapped around his manhood, feeling it throb in her hand. He growled against her mouth, and then hauled her off the desk, his hands on her shoulders forcing her to her knees.

The scent of his male musk filled her nostrils as she engulfed his smooth, hard cock. Her hands stroked his shaft, cupped his heavy, thick-skinned balls. Her tongue traced the ridge of his cockhead, teased the opening and lovingly laved the smooth crown.

Feet planted apart for balance, his hands gripped her head holding her in place, his fingers fisted in her hair.

She sucked hard, moaning hungrily.

"That's it, Jamie. Suck my cock. You're so good," he praised her. His head was thrown back, his eyes closed.

Jamie watched him, loving the expression of painful ecstasy contorting his face, the groans he couldn't control. Her pussy surged with wetness as an idea took root in her mind, something she had never done before. Tucking a hand between her thighs, she lubricated one finger with her juices. Continuing to suck his cock, she reached between his ass cheeks and inserted her finger into his asshole.

"Fuck!" He jerked violently and his eyes flew open.

She held his gaze as she finger-fucked his ass. His muscles clenched spasmodically around her finger, his cock growing harder, larger than ever before.

The shock of pleasure that it brought him ratcheted up her own desire. For the first time she understood what her husband got out of it when he penetrated her anally with his fingers or a sex toy. A powerful thrill of lust raced through her. She relished the involuntary display of emotions that flashed across his face: outraged surprise, helpless lust, masculine vengeance. He would respond in kind, she knew, and the thought inflamed her with fearful pleasure. He had placed her on her knees, but he was at her mercy. For now.

His face contorted as she slowly rotated and pumped her finger inside him. "Damn you, Jamie," he groaned.

Without warning, he yanked her up, spun her around and shoved her, ass-up, over the desk.

"You want to play, Jamie?" he asked threateningly. "I'll play.

How's this?"

His palm barely tapped her bottom, but tender as she was, it sent fiery curls of rapture sizzling through sensitive nerve endings.

"And this?" He lightly spanked the other cheek.

Burning pleasure knifed through her with each gentle slap. Then the knob of his cock was at her cunt, and he surged inside with one powerful thrust.

With the butt plug inside her rectum, his cock filled her pussy to overcapacity. He allowed her no time to adjust to his girth, but thrust long and deep. She felt every hard inch of him, like velvet over hot steel, rasping her clit and tormenting that secret place deep inside.

He grabbed the butt plug and rocked it in her ass, assailing her in both channels now, buffeting her on a sea of raw, sharp sensation. A red-hot primal urge was curling and twisting, driving her to thrust against his cock, the plug. She needed to come so bad it was killing her.

"Oh god-oh-god-oh-god," Jamie moaned in wanton distress. "Help me…." Her hips bucked against him while her fingers clawed at the smooth top of the desk. "Now, Reese, please now."

He pulled out abruptly and removed the butt plug. Her breath caught in her throat as she spied him lubing his erection already slick and glistening from her juices. Her heart hammered. She had to have him inside her. She needed it more than she'd ever needed anything.

She gasped as two broad, long fingers, warm from the heat of his body, and cool from the thick, creamy lube, pressed into her asshole, working the lubricant into her anal passage. Her muscles clenched around the marauding fingers, wanting more.

"Hurry, hurry," she panted.

"Easy, honey, easy." His voice soothed, but his fingers continued to work gently while his ragged breathing betrayed his own need.

Then his fingers were gone, and his erection prodded her

back entrance.

Jamie's hands braced against the desk. In the polished surface, she could see her reflection, her gaze wild with lust and triumphant satisfaction—an expression she could see mirrored on her husband's face.

"Bear down now, sweetheart," commanded her husband.

As he pressed forward, she pushed back, and her mouth opened in a silent gasp of wonder and rapture as her husband's huge cockhead penetrated the place that had been inviolate. She had expected some pain, had steeled herself for it, but instead she was overcome by ecstasy agonizing in itself. Pleasure, pain—she couldn't tell where one ended and the other began. Wider and wider her body opened to him, surrendered to him.

"I can't stand it!" she cried.

"Do you need me to stop?"

"No! More, please more. Fuck me, Reese, please." The sensation of fullness was incredible. His possession shot flames of lust deep into her anal channel, into her womb, her pussy, her clit, her nipples. Her body trembled with the force of her desire. Pleasure and pain merged into one indistinguishable sensation

"That's it. Take my cock, baby. All of it. Open for me, Jamie. That's it." He rocked gently, forward and back, easing into her, until he buried himself to the hilt, his heavy balls pressing against her creaming cunt. She clenched his full length, marveled at having him inside her, The exquisite pressure was so much more than she had envisioned. She felt the thick ridge of his cockhead and every pulse of him. He was impossibly long and massive; there was no place inside her that he wasn't touching.

Open for me sweetheart, he had commanded, and she had. Allowing him access to her body had granted him full access to her heart and soul as well. She belonged to him, physically and spiritually. In releasing her fears, she granted him her ultimate trust, a trust to be held and cherished. She trembled with the intimacy of it.

Reese felt the shudders wracking his wife's slender body. All barriers, physical, emotional and spiritual, shattered. He could sense the difference, feel the emotion that flowed through her. It washed over them both, humbling him. She'd given him the priceless gift of herself.

The sight of their merged bodies, his cock buried inside her, awed him. She was so small, so tight, yet her body accepted him so perfectly. Her tiny puckered entrance had opened, accommodating him easily, readily, and then her muscles had closed around his cock, holding him like a vise, like she never wanted to let him go.

Like he never wanted to let her go.

"Ah, Jamie, what you do to me. You humble me." His cock was throbbing, inpatient, but he overrode its insistent demands, controlled his need to jackhammer into her. He wanted to make her burn, ache, convulse in his arms, but not hurt.

"I'm going to make you fly, sweetheart."

To Jamie's ears, Reese's tone sounded reverent, but tortured. His hands, strong but gentle, held her hips as slowly, he began to thrust, nearly pulling out, before easing back in. He'd prepared her well. Her body was relaxed and lubed, there was no discomfort, only delicious growing pressure as his long length stroked her, caressed her, flooded her senses and washed away all other thoughts except thoughts of him, of his body inside hers. Reese's breathing was hot and heavy, tortured, mirroring her own gasps for air. She felt his body shaking with the superhuman effort it took to control his movements, when the driving, long-denied urges were compelling him to pound into her.

His hands slid up to grasp and tug on each pebbled nipple. Her whimpers of lustful delight turned to moans of unbearable ecstasy as one hand moved between her legs and zeroed in on her clit. Her entire body tensed, flooded by savage, biting need as he manipulated the pulsing organ.

Her body shook with want, her pussy and clit pulsing, her anal muscles squeezing his cock. She felt him throbbing, his control held only by a desperate, thin thread.

"You're going to kill me," Reese groaned. "Now, Jamie. Come for me now," he commanded and sharply smacked her engorged clit.

Shock and rapture knifed through her.

"Now, goddamnit." He kissed her pulsing organ with biting, quick slaps.

Stars burst behind her eyes as an orgasm ripped through her, an explosion of agonizing sensation that seared every nerve ending with a white-hot fire. She heard her own desperate voice crying out, begging, pleading as she was hurled into a maelstrom. The world disintegrated into nothingness, leaving only the all-encompassing rapture. Her fingers clawed at the smooth desktop, her hips bucking. Her clit and pussy contracted in tortured convulsions, and her anal muscles tightened around Reese's cock, milking him.

He roared, a raw, savage sound, and drove into her. "I'm going... to come... in your ass."

With his harsh, guttural utterance, her climax reached its crescendo. She exploded into a fireball of ecstasy at the same time that Reese surrendered to his release, convulsing inside her, pumping his hot seed deep into her body, flooding her with wet heat.

Reese's thrusts didn't stop with his climax, but only slowed, as if he couldn't bear to let her go.

Jamie savored the sensuous slide of his still hard cock. She couldn't speak, was unable to form words. Her body felt weighted while her mind floated, drifting on a wave of euphoria and gratitude.

His stroking finally slowed to a stop, and he rained kisses on the nape of her neck, caressed her breasts. "I don't want to move," he said. "I can't let you go."

"I don't want you to let me go."

Reese groaned.

"I should have trusted you," Jamie said. "I can't believe I denied us this pleasure. I was so stupid—"

"No," he cut her off. "I tried to rush you. That was wrong." He disengaged from her, grabbed his chair and pulled Jamie onto his lap. She curled up in his arms, burying her face in his neck. She recalled her old boss saying Reese demanded a hundred and ten percent. He did indeed. But he gave back a hundred and twenty. Everything she had surrendered to Reese he had returned to her in spades. She had submitted to him, and he had filled her, with his body and his love, his commitment. His indulgence.

Beneath her hand, his heart beat strongly, and she knew it beat for her. Idly, her fingers played with one of his male nipples, enjoying the way it hardened. "Would you get your nipples pierced for me?" she mused aloud.

"Your wish is my command." He smiled. "Do you want me to have it done now?"

Jamie giggled. "Maybe not today. But soon." She sighed in contentment. "Now that I've experienced everything, you might find that I'm insatiable."

Reese laughed. "Oh, you haven't experienced everything, Mrs. Nichols. And as far as you being insatiable, I hope so. Because my desire for you will never be sated."

Starla Kaye

Trusting Her

TRUSTING HER

Sam Caldwell looked down at the cup of coffee slowly growing cold in front of him. Growing cold, like his marriage of late. It was his own damn fault, too. He used to be able to handle everything pretty much on his own. Well, with his handful of reliable ranch hands who he guided along with little or no instruction most of the time. They knew what to do, and he trusted them to do their jobs. But he was the man in charge around the Circle C.

He took a sip of the cool coffee and grimaced. Should have taken a drink sooner. He shouldn't have spent all this time sitting here fretting about the problems in his life like some old woman. Instead he should have more than half-listened to two of the neighboring ranchers with him in the booth of the town's favorite diner.

Saturday mornings generally had him sitting here chatting and bs-ing with a few of the ranchers in the area. This was their time to catch up on not only what was going on with their ranches but also with the sad state of affairs for ranchers in general. He usually chimed in with his opinions.

But today he hadn't said much. He wasn't even all that interested in what was being said. His thoughts kept wandering back to how his wife had stopped smiling around him lately, how she had begun keeping her distance from him. Truth was, his ranch hands were starting to avoid him as well.

"When you going to snap out of this blue funk you've been

in?" Pete asked from across the table. "You've been grouchier than a wounded bear the last month."

His other friend nodded agreement. "You and Katie aren't having problems, are you? I'd sure hate to hear that."

Were they? No, he was the problem. Sam shook his head and abandoned holding onto the cold cup of coffee. He offered a weak excuse for his behavior of late. "If a man had a snippy time of the month like a woman does, then I guess that's what's happening with me. Hell, even I can't stand to be around me right now." That was the truth, too.

His friends chortled and took off talking about the horrors of dealing with their wives when they were PMS-ing. Sam wasn't up to listening to that. He stood to dig coffee money out of his jeans' pocket and set it on the table. They went right on with the current subject of their conversation, how Pete's wife turned into Dragon Woman once a month. Sam counted himself lucky in that moment. His Katie got a little testy at that time of the month, and sometimes he even had to warm her backside to straighten her out, but, all in all, it wasn't so bad.

He grabbed his Stetson from a hook on the wall beside the table and planted it on his head. "See you next week, boys."

"Kiss that sweet wife of yours, let some of her cheery disposition rub off on you," Pete teased as Sam walked through the half-full diner toward the door.

He caught a few more comments about his sour mood of late from some of the other ranchers hanging around and drinking coffee. One man even called out that he needed a swift kick in the butt or something. If he didn't know that the men taunting him actually liked him, he might have stopped to snap at them. But he managed to take their ribbing in stride and headed out to his pickup truck. If he wasn't in a better mood by next week, even his old friends might start steering clear of him. He needed to work through whatever had him going around in a crotchety mood, complaining when there wasn't anything to complain about, snapping at others for no reason. Especially at his wife.

By the time he pulled onto the gravel road leading to his ranch, the sun was high in the sky. It promised to be a real burner for late in May, but then this was Kansas. It could be a burner one day and plumb cold the next this time of year. All you could really count on was the wind, which never seemed to stop. But, as he drove past the heart of the ranch buildings and to his driveway, it wasn't the heat of the day that had him feeling cantankerous and sweaty. No, it was the strange turn of thoughts he'd been mulling over for the last few miles. Really strange. Never would he have imagined himself thinking along this line.

Spanking. He never really gave it much thought except when it was necessary that he turn his wife over his knee for a sound walloping. She had a tendency to get over-tired and then cranky, so he burned her bottom to get her refocused. Sometimes she failed to follow through on a promise she made to him or to one of the community groups she was involved with, so he heated her backside for letting whoever it was down. He'd been spanking her, with her acceptance, since before they'd married. After a spanking her attitude definitely improved, even if she might not sit well for a day or two. The fact that he spanked her for discipline wasn't an issue between them. He loved her and she knew it, even when he reddened her butt.

He pulled into the driveway and turned off the engine. It really hadn't been spanking Katie that he'd been thinking about these final miles. He gripped the steering wheel for a second to rein in his thoughts again. *Can I really do it? Can I humble myself enough to tell Katie I need a spanking?*

His buttocks clenched just at the idea. Did Katie's bottom clench like this when he told her he was going to spank her? He remembered how she usually sucked in a nervous breath and the way her eyes widened in distress and her pretty cheeks turned pink when he brought up the subject. It wasn't a pleasant subject for either of them, or a pleasant experience. But she took her punishment, sometimes with a bit of resistance at first or a weak attempt at protesting. It came back to her knowing he loved her and her trusting him.

He let go of the steering wheel and pressed his lips together in grim determination. Hell, he knew she loved him. And he certainly trusted her. So he damn well needed to stop pondering this issue and just do something about it. A spanking helped his wife when she had attitude problems, so surely it would help him, too.

Determined and a bit anxious about his crazy notion, he got out of his truck. His heart raced, and he took a second to steady his emotions. He stood staring at the log home he and his men had built five years ago. It made him proud to look at it, especially knowing how much Katie loved the place. He'd built it with proposing to her in mind. He'd been in love with her ever since high school when she'd first brought him to his knees with a simple kiss. They'd dated off and on while he went to college at Kansas State University and she went to the University of Kansas. Being separated like that hadn't made a relationship easy. Fact was, relationships were never easy. There had been a time when he'd thought she was drifting away from him, and probably should have because he'd been somewhat of an idiot.

He'd failed them both and gone out one lonely night with one of the cheerleaders. Katie had been spitting mad when he'd guiltily admitted it. She'd gotten so pissed at him, so out of control, that he'd finally bent her over his knee for the first time and spanked the sass right out of her. She'd not spoken to him for two weeks after that. Then she'd come to the frat house where he'd been living and flat out told him they were getting married as soon as they graduated.

He looked toward the kitchen where he was pretty certain she'd be baking something for him. She loved to bake, and she spoiled him and his men something awful. Every one of them had a sweet tooth. No doubt about it, he was a damn lucky man. Lately, though, he knew he wasn't any kind of prize husband-wise. And she sure didn't deserve his sour attitude.

He sucked in a deep breath and bucked up his courage. Maybe when he told her about this one crazy idea she'd run fleeing from the insane man he'd become. But what if she didn't? What if she went along with this wild notion? Could he actually go through with it?

Set one damn foot in front of another and get your sorry ass in the house. Go talk to your wife. Trust in her. All of that was a hell of a lot easier said than done. Yet he forced his legs to move and turned his back to the rest of the ranch, knowing that there were a lot of chores he should be helping with instead of doing this. But if he chickened out and turned around now, he knew he'd never round up the nerve to do this again. *Just keep walking. The chores will get done without you today. You need this.*

Katie hummed along to the country music coming from the radio on the counter across the kitchen. Her heart wasn't actually into the music, though. She'd been worried about Sam when he sped out of the ranch yard this morning on his way into Haverty to have the usual Saturday morning coffee with his buddies. Actually, she'd been worried about him for a while now. He'd gotten this surly and stayed that way for this long one other time in the six years that they'd been married. She'd almost considered leaving him then. She wouldn't consider it this time, she loved him too much. She just needed to find out how to help him out of this mood. If only he'd talk to her about what was bothering him. If only she knew how to ask him about it, without having him snap at her.

She had decided to bake him an apple pie, his favorite dessert. The timer went off on the stove at the same time she heard the familiar sound of Sam's heavy footsteps headed in her direction. Uneasiness flitted through her. The need for her husband to walk into the room, pull her to him, and kiss her silly also filled her. But she doubted that would happen today. It hadn't happened in too long.

She pulled the sizzling pie from the oven as he walked into the kitchen. She heard his appreciative deep inhale of the spicy scent and the way his stomach rumbled. He'd refused breakfast before he'd left for town. It sounded like he hadn't eaten at the diner either.

"Something wrong?" she asked warily, setting the pie on a hot pad on the counter. She knew that he wasn't around the house this time of day, except on Sundays for their usual big noon feast with the ranch hands. She couldn't imagine what had brought him here now, unless…. No, it couldn't be for that reason. She'd been on her best behavior lately.

He met her gaze, looking even more serious than normal. It took him a few seconds, but he finally blurted out, "I need your help with something."

Katie gaped at him, confused. She could count on one hand the number of times he'd asked her for help since they'd said their I-dos. "Sure, of course." She tried to study his expression, but he was even harder to read than usual. "Does this have anything to do with how…with how…well, with how disgruntled you've been lately? With what's bothering you?"

Sam took off his hat and set it brim up on the counter. "Disgruntled, huh? Don't you mean acting like an ass?"

Her blue eyes widened at his bluntness. "You have been a little out of sorts." *Okay, serious understatement.* He'd become almost unbearable to live with.

He leaned against the counter and seemed to struggle with what to say next. His handsome face pinched in frustration until he said, "When you get all grumpy and out of sorts, you get your sweet butt burned."

As always happened when they talked in any way about spanking, her cheeks flamed in acknowledgment. She was a spanked wife, as embarrassing as that was, but she accepted it because she loved her big cowboy husband far more than she disliked being spanked.

He held her gaze and she knew that he, too, was remembering how only a couple of days ago she'd gone over his knee and he'd spanked her bottom until it turned good and red. Not that that was unusual. He spanked her fairly regularly. She tended to get mouthy at times, had a bit more of a temper control problem than he liked, and she could be a little more independent and rebellious than he tolerated. She hated getting spanked at the time, but she easily forgave him when they had their make-up sex later.

Uncomfortable with his continued silence and frown, she pulled the oven mitts from her hand and nervously said, "I haven't done..." She didn't finish the thought, knowing he would understand anyway.

"No, darlin', I'm not here to talk about burning your butt again."

Thank goodness. The tension eased out of her. "Okay, so why are you here? What do you want me to help you with?"

He stood there looking at her as if he didn't know how to continue, as if he wished he'd never walked into the kitchen. She wasn't used to him being this indecisive. She was used to the man who kindly but firmly controlled everything on the ranch and in his household. When she was in trouble, she knew it real fast. He didn't waste much time with lecturing her on the why's. He took her over his knee or bent her over something and fired up her poor bottom. Likewise, when he was in the mood for sex, he didn't waste a lot of time...unless he was in the mood for spending some long, serious time taking her from one orgasm to another. Usually he got right down to business and took her quick and hard. Generally speaking, that was good for her, too.

"Sam, what's going on here? Speak to me."

He thrust his chin out, straightened his shoulders, and stated grimly, "I need you to help me with my attitude problem."

She blinked. "I don't understand."

His expression mirrored frustration. He shifted awkwardly. "What happens when you have attitude issues?"

Katie felt quivers of knowledge in her stomach. Her buttocks tingled in memory. Her cheeks grew heated again, and she said quietly, "You spank me."

"Bingo!" He looked almost joyous that she understood.

She still didn't fully comprehend what he was getting at. "You want *me* to spank you?" Surely she was misunderstanding him.

He glanced away, and she watched color creep up his face. Embarrassed?

"I don't really *want* to be spanked, no," he admitted and she felt relieved. "I need it, though, like you do sometimes. At least I think I do."

"I don't ever *need* to be spanked," she automatically protested, stopping when he raised one eyebrow in challenge.

He let her comment go and studied the scuffed toes of his boots. "Hell, Katie, I don't really know anything except I can't keep going around growling and snapping at everyone. Including you." He looked up, and she saw his incredible love for her in his eyes. "Especially you."

That roundabout apology warmed her. He didn't say he was sorry easily. This had to be tough on him, this humbling himself to come to her with this bizarre request. She chewed her lower lip for a second and finally said, "I'm not sure I can do it, spank you. It even sounds strange. I get spanked, not you."

"Until now." His jaw was set in determination, although his eyes hinted at his wariness.

It was so hard for her to comprehend what he wanted done. *Spanked. He wants me to spank him.* He would never want any of his ranch hands or his friends finding out about this, just as she preferred her being a spanked wife kept private. He was pure Alpha male, dominant, a leader, the head of his house. He turned her over his knee and reddened her bottom when he felt she needed it, not that she'd ever really fought him about it. This talk about punishing him was well beyond "thinking out of the box," as far as she was concerned.

"You love me, right?"

"Of course I do! Maybe you've pushed my nerves lately, but I love you anyway." She knew he wanted an answer, but she couldn't give him one right now. "I need to think, Sam. You can't just spring something like this on me."

Disappointment crossed his face, but he nodded. "I reckon you're right. It boggles my mind a bit thinking about it, too."

"Why don't you go wait in our bedroom while I consider the matter?" The second the question was out of her mouth she wondered if she'd gone too far. She'd been the one sent to their bedroom in the past.

That eyebrow went up again, but he calmly said, "I suppose it's only right that I be sent upstairs to await my fate."

"Like you make me do sometimes. When I have to go fret over what you're going to do: spank me with your hand, thrash me with your belt, or whale at me with the paddle." She nodded and gave a weak smile. "Yes, I guess it's your turn to deal with the whole unpleasant waiting time. Even if I decide that I can't do as you asked." Actually, she kind of liked the idea of sending him to their bedroom to think about being punished. A taste of his own medicine.

"Now that I'm facing this waiting time, I don't really like it. I'm pretty sure you don't like it, either." He heaved a sigh and turned to walk back out of the room. "Am I going to have to wait long?"

He usually made her wait at least a half hour, maybe longer. It was really tempting to let him stew for a good long while, but, as impatient as he could be at times, he was going to get frustrated really fast. "I'll be up in a half hour."

Katie watched her big cowboy husband walk out of the kitchen. Surprised didn't come close to how she felt. Stunned was more like it. Her heart raced at the strange idea. He had a good hundred pounds on her and a good ten inches. He'd crush her if she took him over her knee for a spanking.

Spank him? He wants me to spank him? She slumped against the counter and looked at the apple pie she'd baked him in the hope that his favorite dessert would bring him out of his sour mood. But it wasn't a pie he wanted. He wanted her to spank him. She just couldn't wrap her mind around the concept.

Still... He had been making everyone—including her—

walk on eggshells lately, afraid they'd cross him wrong and get a verbal lashing for no good reason. He hadn't been kissing her, hugging her, or paying her much attention in bed either lately. She certainly missed their normal intimacy. Maybe he really did need a good shaking up, a stern talking to. A spanking.

Her gaze shifted to the pantry where the worn paddle he used at least every couple of months on her poor bottom hung on a hook. Gawd, she hated that paddle. It stung like the dickens, but it taught quite a lesson, too. She sure didn't misbehave in that particular way again anytime soon. If she was going to spank him, the paddle would probably be the best choice. Her small hand sure wouldn't deliver much of a punishment.

Still, could she actually do this? Spank the man who had always been the head of their household, who corrected her misbehavior, who soundly punished her when she broke one of their rules? He was a leader amongst the ranching community. He wore confidence and authority so easily. He gave an order and his men didn't even question it. How could such a man humble himself to let her—to ask her—to spank him?

When he'd walked in the door in the middle of the day, she'd been immediately concerned. She'd started going through everything she'd done in the last few days, trying to determine if he'd shown up out of the blue to punish her for something. And she'd vividly recalled how he'd spanked her the other day for acting sassy about…. In truth, she couldn't even remember now what she'd acted sassy about. It didn't matter. Once he spanked her all was forgiven.

She dug the mixing bowl and beaters out of the sink to put them in the dishwasher. Her gaze landed on the rubber spatula, which made her think about the hard, wide wooden spoon in the drawer. Her buttocks clenched. More than a few times Sam had pulled it from the drawer and given her a few sharp whacks with that nasty spoon. Should she use the spoon on his bare bottom? Let him have that "wonderful" experience?

Okay, she'd obviously decided that she would do as he

asked, since she was now playing around in her mind with what implement she'd use. Her stomach fluttered with nerves not unlike it did when she was the one sent to their bedroom to await punishment. She hated waiting. And she loved her husband enough not to make him wait any longer for her decision.

Determined to do as he asked of her, she went to the pantry and took down the paddle. It was the first time she carried it not because he'd told her to bring it to him, but because she was going to use it *on* him. Her fingers tingled at even holding the paddle. It felt cool to her touch, but she knew from experience it soon turned an equally cool bottom hot.

Walking away from his wife, walking up the stairs and to their bedroom to await her decision had been damn hard. Sam toed off his boots and began pacing the bedroom. What would she decide? At least she hadn't looked at him like he'd become insane. She'd looked shocked, yes, but justifiably so. His idea had shocked him as well, still did. But he would stand behind it and accept whatever choice she made.

He glanced out the window to see several of his ranch hands getting ready to ride out on horseback to do some checking on the cattle in the west field. Normally he'd be riding out with them. Instead he was in this room waiting to find out if his sweet wife loved him enough to spank his ass. *Spank him!* It sounded so odd. He hadn't been turned over someone's knee and had his butt beat in nearly twenty years. And he'd never been spanked by a woman, not even his mother. Could he really do this?

Finally he heard Katie's footsteps coming up the stairs. Thank goodness! He didn't think he could have withstood waiting any longer. He might have to rethink how long he made her wait for punishment in the future.

He tensed and turned to watch her walk into the bedroom. His stomach knotted as he spotted the worn, foot-long wooden paddle from the pantry in her hand. This could be bad. He remembered her crying hard when he gave her a good, firm paddling. Sometimes she even screamed. He was tough, he would keep it together.

"I guess you've made your decision. You're going to punish me." He stood by the window and noted how her shoulders were stiff. Her chin set with determination.

"I decided you wouldn't have asked me to do this if it wasn't really important to you." She moved further into the room, her small hand holding tight to the paddle. "If it's so important to you, then it is to me as well."

He couldn't seem to stop looking at the paddle, much as he remembered her doing before he applied it to her bottom. "I'm hoping it'll improve my attitude, like it tends to do yours. I'm tired of everyone avoiding me. Of being irritated with myself." He walked around the bed and waited for instruction.

"If we're being honest here, then I'll tell you that I'm real tired of your grouching around, too. And I'm even more tired of you coming to bed in a sour mood, turning away from me, and going to sleep without even a goodnight kiss." Her mouth pursed in annoyance at that admission.

Guilt weighed on him. She was right. "I'm sorry, sweetheart."

Her chin ratcheted up a notch. "As you tell me, 'sorry' is an easy word to say, especially when facing a spanking. Meaning it isn't quite so easy." She glanced at the pillows. "Stack a couple of them on the end of the bed. Then you can take those jeans off before you bend over the pillows."

Sam went to get the pillows, thinking about how many dozens of times he'd made her do this little pre-spanking chore. It wasn't easy to do when you knew you'd soon be stretched over them with your butt in the air waiting to be swatted. But he did it, and he pulled off his jeans and tossed them aside. At her simple nod, he drew in a breath and stretched over the pillows. It felt really odd to be in this position, vulnerable. She was in charge now, not him. His gut knotted. It was damn hard to give up being in charge.

She walked next to him and gently folded his shirt tail onto his back, his tighty-whities still covered his butt. Again, he thought about how he sometimes put her in this position, with her panties still on. Sometimes he made her strip completely first. He was glad she hadn't made him do that. This was humiliating enough.

Then with an amazing show of strength, she landed the paddle with a biting Swat! His eyes flashed wide and he gasped, "Shit!"

"The first one is always the worst." She reached down to smooth the sting as he sometimes did. "Now, shall I lecture you about why you're getting spanked? Like you do me."

"I'd just as soon not." He didn't like being in this position now that he was actually here.

She sent another smack to his other butt cheek. "Exactly how I feel when bent over with my bottom up for your undivided attention. That doesn't stop you from reciting everything I've done wrong and why I'm going to get a sound spanking."

He had a feeling she was starting to enjoy this situation. Payback really could be a bitch.

The smooth wood of the paddle settled against his smarting butt and she said, "Okay, let's go over the reasons why you find yourself bent over the bed just now."

Whack! "You've been growling around the ranch for nearly a month."

Whack! "You've been biting my head off for no good reason, otherwise barely even talking to me." Whack!

Sam hissed, "Damn, sweetheart, lighten up a bit."

"Lighten up? Are you kidding me? We've barely even started and you're wussing already!" Clearly annoyed, she nailed his butt hard a dozen times, alternating between cheeks.

He could barely catch his breath. *Shit, shit, shit!*

"Now, where was I?"

Sam glanced awkwardly back and found her standing beside him, holding the paddle. His butt stung like the devil already. "How about you forget the lecturing and just finish up?"

The look she gave him told him he should have kept his mouth shut. She raised the paddle and he turned his head away a second before the hard wood connected with his butt again with a room-echoing whack!

"Shit!" he barked and curled his hands into the quilt.

"Got your attention again, I take it." She smoothed a hand over his blazing bottom. "Heating up nicely."

How many times had he said that to her during a spanking? Too many.

"Okay, one more reason why you're getting spanked and then I'll 'just finish up,' as you suggested." Whack! "Other than make-up sex after you spank me, we haven't had hot and sweaty sex in months." Whack! "And I'm really, really upset about that."

"Katie, I'm sorry," he gritted out. He was, too. "I've been an idiot."

"As you so often say, 'damn right.'"

He started to push up. "I'll get my head on straight. No more grouching around. No more…"

She shoved him back down. "Uh-uh. Not done yet." She went back to turning his ass into a mound of pain. Swat after swat blasted against his butt, never letting up, covering every inch. She must have given him at least a couple dozen whacks with that god-awful paddle.

One sharp whack shot him deeper into the pillows, had him yelling out, "Katie! Stop! Enough!" He sucked in a ragged breath, tears stung his eyes. "I'm sorry as hell. For everything. I'll take you right now. I swear, I'll do anything you want. Just stop."

Sam curled his fingers tighter on the quilt. His teeth were gritted together so hard his jaw hurt. Why the hell had he asked for this? How the hell did she endure it time and time again? His respect for her grew even more.

"So you're truly sorry for your misbehavior? Not just tired of getting your bottom paddled?" She held the wood against his lower cheeks. She questioned him just as he did her, testing to see if he'd had enough. She would stop, he knew that.

If she could take a firmer paddling than this, he sure could. Macho fool that he was. "Do I stop paddling your butt with your first pleas and promises?"

The paddle lifted and she sighed. "No. You paddle me until I'm wriggling all over the pillows. Until my legs are kicking up and I'm swearing on my life never to misbehave again. Sometimes until I'm sobbing my heart out."

He sure didn't want to do any of that, but he couldn't show weakness yet. He was tougher than she was. "Then I guess you'd better start swinging that paddle again."

To his surprise she set the paddle on the bed next to him. Then she said, "It's time I pulled these shorts down and bared that bottom of yours."

Bared his bottom! Sure, he did that to her, should have expected this was coming. But hell! His face heated. This was damn embarrassing. It took all his inner control to stay in position over the pillows and raise up on his toes enough that she could tug his undershorts down to his knees. He looked straight ahead at the headboard. His face flamed almost as much as his ass at the humiliation of what she'd done, of his vulnerability. He never thought anything of doing this to her. A spanking was best delivered on the bare.

She picked up the paddle and repeated what he'd told her many times. "The most memorable spankings are delivered to a bare butt, or so I'm told on a regular basis." She leaned down to kiss one burning ass cheek. "Pretty embarrassing, isn't it?"

"I have to admit it is. It doesn't mean I won't still be doing it to you in future spanking sessions." But he'd appreciate her acceptance of his insistence on doing so more next time.

The loud Whack! of the paddle shot him forward into the pillows and had him sucking in a breath. He guessed she didn't like him talking about "future spanking sessions."

"Hold on tight, cowboy. I'm getting ready to make sure you don't sit well in the saddle or anywhere else for at least a day." She rained a quick shower of swats that proved she was serious.

"Damn, woman!" he bit out, curling his toes into the carpet.

The swats kept right on coming until she said, "My arm is getting tired."

"My ass is near worn out." He was more than ready for her to stop.

But she didn't, she evidently found a new source of strength because she went back to blazing up the fire already flaming on his ass. "I'm doing this until you tell me to stop. Or until I think you've had enough."

Tell her to stop! Do it! You won't sit for a week if she keeps this up. Idiot that he was, he refused to break so easily. *Easily?* He remained silent, except for panting between swats.

Then it happened, to his horror. He kicked a leg up at the knee, then stomped down hard at the miserable pain from one particularly hard swat.

He didn't quit a spanking, though, just because she kicked her legs. She wasn't broken at that point. And they'd both agreed years ago that if he was going to spank her, he would do it until she'd taken all she could. She needed to learn whatever lesson was being taught well enough that she couldn't fail it again for a long time. She didn't give up on him now either.

The damn paddle kept right on landing against his throbbing butt. Finally he blinked back a tear, again to his horror. Then he felt one trickle down his face at the same time he shot forward and deep into the pillows, yelling out, "Okay! Stop! Dammit, stop!"

He sensed the paddle still held up in the air and he vowed painfully, "I'll apologize to everyone on the ranch if that's what you want. I'll make love to you three times a day. Anything! Just stop!"

To his relief, Katie immediately backed away. She didn't say a word for several seconds. He couldn't talk anyway. Holy Hell he hurt!

"You should probably stay there for a while longer," she said, sounding uncertain about telling him that.

Now that she'd done as he'd asked, as he'd practically

begged her to do, she seemed worried about his reaction. Truth was, he didn't really look forward to getting up at the moment. Not that he liked lying in this embarrassing position with his red ass on display. Again, that made him realize all that he asked of her when he paddled her sweet butt.

He closed his eyes and blinked away the remaining moisture in them. He sure didn't want her seeing tears. "How long do you want me to stay here?" he asked, trying to let her know that she was still in charge and that he was okay with it. But he really just wanted her to leave him be for a bit so he could come to terms with the fierce pain.

"Ummm, ten minutes?" She remained hesitant.

"Yeah thirty minutes sounds about right." He didn't think he'd be able to pull his darn jeans on any sooner than that. His butt felt swollen, every freaking inch of it.

"Well, okay." He heard her moving toward the doorway, but she stopped to add, "I think this is where I'm supposed to tell you that you're forgiven for your bad behavior."

Sam tried to crane his head around to look at her and even that small movement had him flinching. Shit. Yet he found the grace to say, "This is where I tell you how sorry I am. And I am, darlin', real sorry."

Her gaze was focused on his naked rear propped up in the air, red and throbbing. He knew exactly what she was seeing. She gave him a gentle smile, one filled with so much love that it humbled him even more than getting soundly paddled.

"Not pretty, is it? You've got a wicked arm on you, Katie." In spite of his pain, he was damn proud of her. He knew she hadn't wanted to do this, but she'd done it anyway. He wasn't sure he'd ever want to go through this again, but, he supposed, time would tell.

Katie's smile turned up a notch and tipped at the edge with amusement. "It's kind of nice to be on the other side of this spanking thing. Besides, you've deserved a good paddling for a while now."

He shifted slightly once more and groaned before he could

control it. Her smile disappeared, and she started toward him, but he shook his head. "No, not yet. No comforting just yet. I need to have some time alone to deal with what happened."

She stopped, looking at him in understanding. "Pretty tough on your supreme machoness, wasn't it? Bruised your ego a little. But you'll get beyond this pain. I'm sure in no time at all you'll be back to strutting around here like the Super Stud you are."

Sam gave her a wobbly grin. "Hard to feel all 'supreme macho' after having been soundly paddled by my loving wife. Or like 'Super Stud' with my ass on fire and sticking up in the air." Still, his cock was starting to perk to life from where it was pressed into the pillows. "I might not be able to fully earn the title of 'Super Stud' until tonight, darlin'."

The plump breasts he so loved to caress and suckle rose and fell in her growing arousal. Her eyes heated. "Looking forward to it, cowboy."

She pulled the bedroom door closed with a final, "I'll let you alone now to pout in private."

"I'm not going to pout," he countered. He collapsed against the pillows and heaved a shuddery sigh. Getting spanked was not easy to deal with. No sir, his ass was in pure misery.

***

Katie had been keeping herself busy in the kitchen, trying to come to terms with what she'd done to Sam. She'd actually spanked him. It still seemed surreal, but her arm hurt from swinging the paddle so long. Did his arm ever hurt after spanking or paddling her?

She thought about how red his bottom had been when she'd stopped. It had to hurt, a lot. *Been there, had that bottom.* She sympathized, somewhat. In truth, he'd deserved the spanking, and she was pleased that she'd had the nerve to actually give it to him. But now she was worried about him. She didn't like for anyone to suffer, and he would, even if he wouldn't admit it. He had chores to get to yet today. No, it wouldn't be any fun at all doing his chores and having his jeans rubbing against his tender bottom.

She was so lost in thought that she didn't hear her husband come into the room. When his hands settled on her shoulders as she looked out the kitchen window, she jumped. "You startled me. I thought you were still upstairs."

"Finished my spell of pouting." He lifted her hair to nuzzle her neck. "Thought maybe I should start following through with my promises. Like making love to my wife."

His kissing her neck always made her weak in the knees. She sighed. "Your chores…"

He rubbed against her from behind, nudging between her legs with his very hard, very long cock. "Chores can wait. You're more important, and I've been neglecting you. Gotta make up for that now."

She turned in his arms and snuggled into him, pleased that he was now naked from head to toe. With a sassy grin, she reached around to put her hands on his bottom. "Naughty boy got his butt spanked. It's still warm."

He grinned down at her. "Still sore as hell, too." Then he took her hand to tug her with him. "Naughty boy wants to take his naughtiness to a whole new level. You up for that?"

Katie laughed, heart racing. "If this is how you're going to act after a spanking, I just might have to do it more often."

"I'm hoping it won't have to happen very often." He pulled her faster toward the bedroom.

She hesitated and he stopped to look back at her. "So you'd let me spank you again?" It still amazed her.

His expression turned serious. "I love you, sweetheart. I burn your bottom when I think you need it. Guess it wouldn't be right if I didn't accept a spanking from you now and then."

She smiled and then kissed him. "Make-up sex. Now!"

Cara Bristol

Secret Desires

Secret Desires

Morgan Moran adjusted her fuchsia baby doll top to expose her modest cleavage and her pierced navel. Once it was arranged to her satisfaction, she wove through the candlelit tables to a corner booth where Jack waited. Even in the dim flicker cast by the candles, she could tell he was annoyed. His shoulders were bunched with tension, and his fingers drummed on the table as he scanned the restaurant. When his eyes zeroed in on her, his jaw clenched. Morgan's stomach fluttered with uncertainty. She hoped he wasn't going to spoil their night out.

She slid across the leather seat and brushed a kiss against the stern slash of his mouth. "I'm a little late. Have you been here long?" She peered at him through lowered lashes, praying he wasn't going to make a big issue of her tardiness. She had a darn good reason for being late and besides that, she was worth waiting for.

"I tried to call you. You didn't answer your cell." Jack took a sip of his vodka tonic.

"I couldn't. Ramon gets testy when people talk on the phone while he's working."

"Ramon?" Jack's eyebrows rose.

"My hairdresser." Ramon was an artist with the temperament to match. Morgan's golden highlights had desperately needed his creative TLC, but Ramon had been booked weeks out.

It had been a stroke of luck when the salon called with a

cancellation. Before she had known it, it had been time to meet Jack, but she'd still had foils in her hair.

Yes, she was late, but it wasn't like it was her fault.

"Ah." Jack stirred his drink. "Your hairdresser. What else could you have done?" He glanced at his drink, then back at her face. "You look beautiful, by the way. But you always do."

Morgan beamed. Jack understood. He always did. His gentleness, acceptance, and loving nature were his best traits.

A veterinarian with his own clinic, he never turned away a sick animal whose owner couldn't afford to pay. In his spare time, he volunteered at a local animal shelter. His kindness for others had melted a little soft spot in her heart, even though Jack wasn't her usual type.

Morgan always had had a stomach-fluttering weakness for bad boys, emotionally unavailable men with commitment issues or users who discarded her after they got what they wanted.

She'd met Jack when she took her agitated cat, Mr. Whiskers, to his veterinary office for a recurring hairball problem. She had been captivated by the gentle way he calmed Mr. Whiskers' fears. Weary from having her heart broken repeatedly, she had been ready for a gentleman like Jack.

When he'd asked her out, she'd accepted. They had dated for six months before they'd moved in together. That had been a year ago.

Then Morgan had discovered that Jack's gentleness, acceptance, and loving nature were his most irritating traits.

When she got cranky with PMS, he rubbed her back and brought her chocolate. When she forgot to pick up the dry cleaning like she promised, he did it instead. When she burned dinner, he took her out to eat. Every time he did something nice, rather than make her grateful, it made her feel bitchy. She didn't understand it.

She loved him and knew he loved her. Recently he'd hinted about making their relationship permanent, but Morgan wasn't ready for the big M. She worried that in a few years she would crave more excitement than Jack could deliver.

"You ignored me so you wouldn't upset your hairdresser." His eyes sparked.

"Jack!" Morgan gaped at him. "I had *bleach* on my hair!"

"I've been here for an hour, wondering if you were injured in a traffic accident."

"I'm sorry. I should have called." Morgan tried to sound contrite. She bowed her head. She was a teensy bit late. Why was he was making a federal case of this?

A vein pulsed in his temple. "You always say you're sorry, and promise to do better, but you never do."

Morgan pressed a palm to her fluttering stomach. All she wanted was to have a nice romantic dinner, and he was scolding her like she was a naughty child. What was next? Was he going to ground her for a week? Take away her television privileges? She lifted her chin in defiance. "You act like I'm late all the time."

"You *are* late all the time!"

Morgan flushed. "I don't mean to be. Something always comes up." Between her job, volunteering with foster care children, and selling antique buttons on eBay, there weren't enough hours in the day. She was always rushing, careening from one appointment to the next.

"You're never late for work."

"Of course not. I'd get fired." Her boss at the plumbing supply company where she was office manager and bookkeeper was a stickler for punctuality. First offense, you got a warning. Second offense, he docked your pay. Third offense, you were out.

"Were you late to your appointment with Ramon?" His tone held an edge.

She flushed. "That's different."

The waiter arrived with menus, but Jack waved them aside. "She'll have the Caesar salad with chicken. I'll have the steak, medium. Baked potato. Butter, sour cream, no chives."

Morgan's eyes narrowed. She wasn't sure she liked him ordering for her. She wanted a take-charge man, but she was capable of choosing her own meal. "Maybe I want a menu."

He drained the remainder of his drink and peered at her over the glass. "Maybe you should have arrived an hour ago." His tone reminded her of a bulldog refusing to give up a bone.

"I explained that."

"All I know is that when there are consequences, you tow the line." He set down the glass and regarded Morgan steadily. "I love you, and I want to spend my life with you, but your rudeness pisses me off. It hurts when you treat other people—your boss, your hairdresser—better than you treat me."

"That's not true!" She shook her head.

"I'm not going to put up with it anymore. The next time you're late, Morgan…there will be consequences."

Something almost sexual fluttered within her, but annoyance overruled it. She'd wanted him to act more forceful, more authoritative, more macho, but he was pushing it now. She rolled her eyes. "Like what?"

"I'll paddle your ass!"

Shock ricocheted through her, and she fought to control her reaction. She didn't know what surprised her more—that he'd made such an uncharacteristic outburst or that the idea of his hand striking her bottom had her stomach clenching, not in fear, but in arousal. She took slow, even breaths. "You won't do that," she said, unsure if she was stating a fact or challenging him.

"Try me." The cocksure glint in his eyes *was* a dare and her anger ignited, overriding her quickening desire. He had no right to treat her like a disobedient child. He wasn't the boss of her!

She glared at him, but her anger drained away when she realized he would never lay a finger on her. He wasn't the physical type. But instead of relief, she felt strangely disappointed.

***

A wild flame ignited and flickered in Morgan's eyes in a way that Jack Hudson hadn't seen in a long time. He could almost feel the heat. Even though the flash of emotion lasted only moments, his optimism flared. Had Morgan found the idea of a spanking erotic? He adored Morgan, but sometimes she frustrated him. Her lateness this evening was one of those times. He had threatened to spank her to get her attention, to make her realize her behavior was disrespectful. Her eyes widened in shock and a sharp desire surged through him. He could picture Morgan's smooth, rounded, naked bottom turning pink and warm. He imagined the little noises she would make, sounds mimicking cries of passion, and his cock throbbed.

A smile tickled the corner of his mouth. Morgan was her own woman, independent, willful. She wouldn't readily submit to any authority or discipline, but Jack didn't want to dominate her, he wanted to push her buttons.

Lately, he'd been assailed by a strange longing, not dissatisfaction exactly, but a need for something different. When he had threatened to discipline her, for a heart-stopping moment, he would have sworn he'd seen a similar need reflected in her stormy gaze. Her eyes had darkened, glowing hot. But in a flash, the heat had dissipated, leaving him to wonder if it was just wishful thinking on his part.

Disappointment made him want to pound the table.

He and Morgan enjoyed a frequent, boisterous—but nonetheless tame—sex life. Jack yearned to push the envelope.

However, he wouldn't do it without her wholehearted consent and participation. His shoulders bunched in frustration. Unfortunately, Morgan would never give it. She was flirtatious, not kinky.

Once, in jest, Jack had playfully spanked a former girlfriend. He'd barely tapped her jean-clad behind. She'd reacted as if he'd beaten her. He'd apologized profusely, but he'd been unable to regain her trust and soon after, they'd broken up.

He couldn't risk losing Morgan.

Jack glanced at her now. Her mouth was pursed in a pout, her spine ramrod straight. Everything about this woman made him crazy. Crazy with love, crazy with lust. Even angry, she was sexy as hell. Anger released the spitfire nature that he loved so much.

None of that excused her rudeness.

She'd sashayed in an hour late wearing ass-hugging skinny jeans, wet-dream-inspiring high-heeled boots, and a flimsy top that exposed more of her perky breasts than it covered. As she had crossed the restaurant floor, male heads had turned to watch. Every man in the restaurant probably wanted to fuck her. Knowing that turned him on. Picturing it happening excited him more.

He sighed, realizing that would never be. He loved Morgan's confidence, her spunk, her uninhibited expression. He loved that she kept him on his toes.

He hated that she kept him waiting.

Jack stifled a sigh. It didn't matter if they were going to his parents' house, a movie, to dinner, to a party — she ran late. With him. She was more punctual with other people.

Sometimes it seemed like she *wanted* to annoy him. She'd toss her tousled golden hair and her blue eyes would turn beguiling as she rationalized her rudeness. He usually caved – but not today. He was fed up.

Morgan was loving, caring. And self-centered. A little discipline might readjust her attitude. It might anger her, but wasn't makeup sex always the hottest? And what if he was correct about the hint of desire in her eyes? What if the idea of a spanking had turned her on? Perhaps it could lead to something more…

He'd have to approach her carefully, wait for the right time, but domestic discipline might be what their relationship needed.

Jack smothered a grin. He was actually looking forward to the next time she was late.

***

When their food arrived, Morgan attacked her salad with the fork. She wanted to hate it, but the marinated chicken was grilled to perfection, the crisp romaine lettuce coated with the right amount of tangy dressing. Okay, Jack got the meal right. That didn't prove anything. He thought he knew her, but he didn't.

Jack was tucking into his steak with enjoyment. "How's your salad?" he asked, oblivious to her resentment.

"Fine."

"Glad to hear it."

"How's your steak?" she asked sullenly.

"Perfect."

"Glad to hear it," she mimicked.

He set down his knife and fork and covered her hand with his. "Let's not fight. Truce?"

Her irritation vanished at the open, apologetic expression on his handsome face. She acted like such a bitch sometimes. It was a miracle he had stuck around and waited for her. None of her previous boyfriends would have. They would have been long gone.

She sighed. "Truce."

He leaned over and kissed her lightly on the mouth. "I love you," he said.

Warmth settled in her chest and curled in the pit of her stomach. "I love you, too." For a long moment they smiled stupidly at each other, and then Jack reached out and tucked a strand of hair behind her ear.

"Next Saturday is your birthday," he said.

"Don't remind me," she said dryly. It was the big three-oh. The big ugly, nasty three-oh. She would be officially old.

"I thought you'd like a little pampering, so I made an appointment for you at Soma Day Spa."

"For what, a massage, a facial?"

He shrugged. "For whatever you choose. Get the works if you want."

Morgan threw her arms around him. "Thank you. That's a wonderful birthday present."

"I have another surprise, but you'll have to wait."

"What is it?"

He tweaked her nose. "It's a surprise."

A lead weight settled in Morgan's stomach. There were good surprises like a day at the spa, and bad surprises like an engagement ring. What would she do if he popped the question? She didn't want to lose him—she loved him. But, she wasn't ready to get married. Living with a man was one thing—committing to a lifetime of…*niceness* was something else.

Take their sex life. Jack was tender and caring, and she had frequent, pleasant orgasms. But orgasms shouldn't be pleasant. They should be body and soul-shattering. Searingly hot. Explosive.

Sometimes she craved raw, raunchy sex. Jack would be shocked by her yearnings: fucking as other people watched, a threesome with two men, anal sex. She'd once broached the subject with Jack, tentatively feeling him out about the latter and he'd responded that he respected her too much to *do that.*

Do it to me! She had wanted to shout at him.

That, she realized, was the crux of her ambivalence. It wasn't that Jack was too nice. Rather, their sex life was too nice. And she'd heard that sex dwindled over the course of a marriage. She feared she'd shrivel up and die if they only had Saturday night missionary sex after the evening news.

Physically, Jack was smokin' hot. He was tall and broad-shouldered with a thick mat of springy, coarse chest hair that arrowed down to an awesome cock. Thick and long, it was straight as a rod of steel and had an exceptionally speedy recovery time that was woefully underutilized. Jack was a Clark Kent who didn't recognize that he was Superman.

Despite their lackluster sex life, she was crazy about him. She glanced at him now and her heart skipped a beat. She loved his lopsided grin, his sexy green eyes, the rough stubble on his jaw, even his dorky, almost military haircut. Too conservative for her tastes at first, she'd grown to like it. Especially when she fantasized an army soldier was subjecting her to a strip search.

Spread your legs, Miss.

Yes, sir, sergeant!

Whew! She delicately fanned her face.

"Are you okay?" Jack frowned.

"What?"

He pressed a cool hand to her forehead. "You look flushed. You're not getting sick are you?"

"It's just warm in here."

***

Morgan's fingers twined with Jack's as he escorted her to her car. Inside the underground parking structure exhaust tinged the hot, muggy air. Her floor was deserted, but a far-off squeal of tires and the revving of motors created a distant din. They stopped beside her little convertible.

"Do you want a ride to your car?" she asked

"No, thanks. I need to stretch my legs. I'll see you at the house."

Morgan looked at him, and the air seemed to sizzle. An odd tension gnawed at her nerves. She felt as tightly wound as the turbo-charged engine in her sports car. Jack leaned close to peck her cheek, and Morgan flung her arms around his neck, plastering her body against his muscled form. Their lips met, and Morgan put everything she had into the kiss. She teased his lips with her tongue, tracing the outline before slipping inside his mouth. He tasted like warm, earthy male and the Boston cream pie he'd had for dessert, a heady, spicy, sweet mix.

His hands smoothed over her ass, curving her into the cradle of his hips. Her inner yearning grew more insistent. As her desire grew, so did another compulsion, one she couldn't name or understand. All she knew was it was egging her on, propelling her to do…something. Prove something? Morgan cupped Jack's jaw with one hand, the other zeroing in on a flat male nipple. She stroked the hardening bud through the fabric of his shirt.

Jack broke off the kiss to trail his lips down her neck, and Morgan's head fell back. She sucked in a gasp of air, and the acrid odor of the garage filled her senses. On another floor, a car honked. It was smelly, awkward and risky, but the very openness of the venue ignited a burst of fire in her gut. Desire curled in her womb as he caressed her sensitive skin with his lips and teeth. He nipped gently and liquid heat pooled between her legs.

Her top slipped off her shoulder, and his lips were there to explore the bared skin. His hands stroked her bra-covered breasts, rolling the nipples between his fingers. After he divested the strap of her top from her other shoulder, his head lowered and he captured a pebbled nipple through her lacy bra. His mouth was hot and wet, and Morgan needed him to touch her without the barrier of clothes. She released the clasp of her front closure bra, exposing her breasts. Jack drew a nipple into his mouth, but his touch was too gentle.

"Suck hard." Her fingers curled into his hair.

He increased suction slightly.

Her back arched. "More Jack. Suck hard, please."

He pulled hard and deep and her clit pulsed, a torrent of need flooding her. He cupped her mound, pressing against the center of her desire and her hips began to move. She fantasized there were people in the parked cars watching them, and lust wracked her body. Blood coursed through her veins, her heart hammered. Her legs wobbled. Her pussy ached.

The squeal of tires grew louder. Her hands stroked Jack's rock-hard cock through his pants. She wanted him to take her there in the dirty, smelly garage where anyone could catch them.

His fingers released her zipper then eased inside the tight confines of her jeans to stroke her through the wet fabric of her silky, slinky thong. Morgan gasped, falling against the fender of her car. His fingers slid under her thong to toy with her neat, trimmed curls before slowly circling her clit. Her body was coming undone, turning to jelly.

She cried out in feral need, spreading her legs as wide as she could.

"Yeah, man. Fuck her now. Yeah, Baby!" hooted rough male voices. The lewd, lascivious catcall spiked her excitement into a blaze so white-hot, searing pleasure scorched her body. She jerked violently, crying out as her clitoris convulsed, her cunt contracting in forceful spasms.

"No!" she cried in a protest as Jack yanked his hand out of her pants. With his body, he shielded her from view. Morgan heard the men continuing to shout lewd suggestions as the vehicle squealed away, honking raucously.

This is what she had craved. This unfettered, raw, no-holds-barred sexual abandon.

But Jack, nice Jack, had stopped. Morgan stifled a scream of frustration. Release had been so close!

Jack tugged her shirt back into place, covering her breasts. "I'm sorry, Morgan. I don't know what came over me."

"Don't be sorry." She swayed toward him, wanting to continue, but he grabbed her arm.

"You'd better fix your clothes." His gaze shifted to her unzipped jeans, her unhooked bra bunched under her shirt.

How could he do this to her? This was the hottest thing that had ever happened between her and Jack, and she'd been unceremoniously wrenched from the precipice of what might have been a truly mind-blowing orgasm. With jerky movements, she refastened her bra and then zipped her pants. Her folds felt hugely swollen, her clit throbbing the way her finger did the time she'd slammed it in the drawer. And damn near as achy. Men weren't the only ones who felt physical pain when their desire was frustrated! Couldn't Jack tell how turned on she was? How close to coming? Why couldn't he want the same things she wanted? She didn't need him to protect her; she needed him to fuck her. Couldn't he get down and dirty once?

Jack placed a light kiss on her mouth. "That was a close one. In another few minutes they might have really gotten something to whoop it up about."

She bit her lip. "That would have been bad?"

He shook his head. "That's no way to treat the woman I want to spend my life with."

***

Jack worked off his frustration on the road, taking the long way home. If those men hadn't interrupted, he would have fucked Morgan in the garage. He thought he'd overcome his baser urges, but apparently you could take the beast out of the jungle, but you couldn't take the jungle out of the beast. Morgan had only wanted to apologize for her tardiness, but he'd allowed her exuberance to push him over the edge.

He had to force himself to remember that Morgan was the kind of girl you took home to meet mom, that you married, that bore your children, that you grew old with. Not the kind you fucked in a frickin' parking garage just because she was hot and you wanted her so bad you feared your balls would explode.

As much as he wanted a woman who was one and the same—a girl to marry and that he could get kinky with—he knew she didn't exist. History and experience had proven that.

Jack was thirty-five, light-years from the randy young man he'd once been. He could never do with Morgan what he used to do in the old days. He couldn't imagine her screaming in pleasure as he and a buddy took turns fucking her before teaming up and taking her together.

Okay, he did imagine it. It made him hard, kept him awake nights. But he couldn't treat her that way if he expected to have a future with her. He couldn't even bring himself to talk to her about it, afraid she would reject not only his suggestions, but him, too.

He should stop obsessing about what he couldn't have and be satisfied with PB & J. That's how he thought of their sex life—it was a peanut butter and jelly sandwich. It took the edge off his appetite, but it didn't fulfill his real hunger. Like switching from grape to strawberry jam or from smooth to crunchy peanut butter, their sex life varied a little, but it was still basically the same.

PB & J wasn't the kind of sandwich he craved.

It shamed him that his first instinct in the garage wasn't to shield her, but to rip off her jeans and fuck her as strange men cheered.

Lust had exploded inside him like a geyser when they'd been caught and his body's need had nearly driven him to complete the act. But he'd felt Morgan's withdrawal, her shame when she'd cried out, her body recoiling. That confirmed his fantasies had to remain just fantasies.

He would have to get his lascivious urges under control. He would marry Morgan and be happy, damn it.

***

The esthetician was pressing strips of cloth to her nether region, which had been painted with hot wax, as Morgan's cell phone jangled Girls Just Want to Have Fun.

She glanced at the number and answered it. "Hi, Savannah, what's up?"

"Morgan, where are you?" Her friend's voice hissed.

"I'm at the spaAAAAAH." Morgan shouted as the esthetician ripped off the strip and a swath of pubic hair.

"Why aren't you here?"

"Where's here?" Morgan braced herself for the next strip.

"Your house."

"Why are you calling from my house? And why do you sound like you're in a tunnel?"

"I'm in the bathroom," Savannah whispered. "I don't want Jack to hear me. You'd better come home."

"What time is it—MOTHER OF GOD!" She shouted as more hair was torn out. It felt like the technician had taken her skin with it.

"Eet only hurts zee wurst zee first time. Zen it only hurts a lot," the esthetician joked in an accent Morgan couldn't place.

"It's five o'clock," Savannah answered. "What the hell is going on there?"

"I'm getting a Brazilian. It's a surprise for Jack."

"A Brazilian? You can hardly stand to pluck your eyebrows.

And speaking of Jack, he was expecting you an hour ago."

"I'm almost done. I had the works: a full-body massage, manicure, pedicure, facial, detoxifying herb wrap and now a pussy wax."

"Everybody's here, Morgan!"

"What do you mean?"

The esthetician pulled off another strip, and Morgan laughed through the pain. "Ow. That hurts so much."

"Everybody." Savannah said and went silent.

"Are you still there?"

"Jack will kill me if he knows I told you, but he planned a surprise birthday party. Your friends are here, your sister, some people from your work. Jack is acting cool, but he's pissed. I think you're in big trouble."

Ever since the evening in the parking garage, Jack had been different. More intense. Every time they were in the same room together the air seemed to sizzle with an electric tension, although to the outside viewer everything would appear to be normal. But Morgan knew it wasn't. Lightening was going strike. And she didn't want to be there when it did.

"I'm scared," she admitted.

"Of what? Jack is mad, but he'd never hurt you."

"I know that." She paused. "I'm afraid he's going to ask me to marry him."

"I thought you loved him!"

"I do love him. But…" She glanced at the esthetician and shrugged. She was lying on a table, naked from the waist down in front of a complete stranger who'd probably heard it all before. "…But, the sex is boring," she continued. "And, I'm afraid it will only get worse if we get married."

"So spice it up! Go wild on him. He'll love it. But get your butt over here."

"Jack doesn't go for wild."

"Honey, every man goes for wild. And, Jack loves you. He'll want what will make you happy."

***

Morgan crept into the house, closing the front door quietly. A strange clinking sound and a rumble of male voices emanated from the rear of the house. She finger-combed her hair to fluff it, then tugged at the neckline of her tank top, stopping short of exposing her nipples. Taking a deep breath, she followed the noise and tiptoed to the sunroom.

A HAPPY BIRTHDAY MORGAN banner stretched across the wall of the room decorated with colorful helium-filled balloons and streamers. Plates of half-eaten food and used clear plastic cups littered card tables covered with bright, cheery cloths.

Amid the birthday detritus, Jack and three men hunched over a beer-bottle laden folding table beneath a haze of cigar smoke. They clutched playing cards and toyed with stacked poker chips.

She stood hands on her hips, her mouth agape. *This* was her party? Why was Jack playing poker? Why were they smoking cigars in the house? Where was Savannah? Everyone else?

Jack didn't even glance at her. He puffed on his cigar and blew out stream of smoke. "When you were fifteen minutes late, I apologized to your friends." He organized the cards in his hand. "When you were thirty minutes late, the party started without you."

He discarded a card and signaled the dealer for a replacement. "When the guest of honor still hadn't arrived after two hours, everyone gave up and went home. The guys and I decided to play poker so the evening wouldn't be a total waste."

"I'm sorry," she said in a small voice. "I didn't know you had a party planned."

"You knew I had *something* planned." He set his cigar in the ashtray. "Do you remember our discussion about consequences?"

He'd threatened to paddle her. She hadn't taken it seriously. And still didn't. But she was glad the guys were here as a buffer. Otherwise there would probably be a big argument and her birthday would be ruined.

She glanced at Jack's three friends. Arnie, a balding, paunchy middle-aged guy, lived next door. Dean was a veterinarian like Jack. He was in his mid 40s, and newly divorced. Both men were quiet and kind of boring, but they were always pleasant and cordial to her.

Then there was Matt. He and Jack had been buddies since high school. An undercover cop, he cultivated a perpetual three-day growth of stubble and an air of insolence. He'd never said anything impolite, but something about him put her on edge. While Arnie and Dean were studying their cards as if gleaning the secrets to the universe, Matt appeared to relish the tension, his smirk more pronounced than usual.

Jack tossed several chips into the center of the table.

Arnie and Dean folded. "Too rich for me," Dean said.

Matt matched Jack's chips. "Call it."

"Full house." Jack flipped over three aces and two tens.

"Shit," Matt slapped his cards down. "Pair of kings."

Jack scooped up his winnings and collected the scattered cards. He shuffled the deck, then fanned it out. "Pick one, Morgan."

She eyed him suspiciously. Cautiously, she extracted a card and handed it to him without looking at it.

He set it face down on the table and tapped it with his finger. "This is the number of spanks you'll receive for each hour you were late."

Morgan's breath caught in her throat. Her knees went weak, her stomach clenched and her traitorous, newly waxed pussy let down a gush of moisture. She shouldn't be turned on by his commanding tone, by the thought of submitting to his authority, by imagining how it would feel to be spanked.

Her breathing quickened. *No!* She forced aside the erotic thoughts. There would be no spanking. He'd never go through with it. And besides, she wouldn't allow it. She had to show him he couldn't order her around. But what if…

Jack flipped over the card. "Oh, Sweetheart, that's not good."

He shook his head in mock sympathy. "Ace of hearts. Eleven."

Her stomach flip-flopped. "It also counts as one."

"It's my game, so it's eleven. For three hours late, you've earned thirty-three."

"Yeah, right." Sarcasm slipped from her lips. The cards could number sixty-six, and it wouldn't matter. Meek, mild, good-natured-even-if-currently-pissed-off Jack would no more touch her than he would fly to the moon. His threat was all show. She should feel relieved, but instead she felt like a little girl staring at a huge, gaily wrapped present on Christmas morning knowing that it contained only bedroom slippers. Disappointed, she started for the kitchen.

"Where do you think you're going?" Jack's low commanding voice stopped her in her tracks.

She tossed a glance over her shoulder. "I'm going to get something to eat."

He shook his head. "Go wait for me in the bedroom."

"What? Why?" She turned.

"Because I'm going to spank you." Jack's eyes glowed with a dangerous glint. Morgan's knees trembled and her mouth went dry. Could he really be serious? Her heartbeat sounded like a drum in her ears. Or maybe it sounded so loud because the room had fallen into silence. The low hum of masculine conversation had died. The card shuffling had stopped. The clinking of poker chips had ceased.

Arnie focused on the wall as if reading an eye chart, and Dean had found something incredibly fascinating about his shoes. Only Matt appeared unfazed. He relaxed in his chair, his posture casual. The smirk was back in evidence and his gaze was lit by a carnal gleam. He was obviously enjoying the interchange. Morgan recalled rumors that Matt and his girlfriend Janine enjoyed an open, somewhat kinky, relationship. Did he spank Janine? She wondered.

Morgan should have felt mortified that her boyfriend was threatening to discipline her. Instead a pang of sexual longing skittered though her. Her nipples were hardening to thick points, beading through two layers of clothing. Morgan took a deep breath, thrusting out her chest, and watched as Jack's gaze—and Matt's—shifted to her breasts. She smothered a triumphant grin. She'd show Jack who was in control. Her hands settled on her hips. "What if I refuse?"

"Then you've demonstrated that you're not committed to our relationship. You broke another promise. Submit to a spanking or find yourself another man to wrap around your finger."

Morgan gaped at him. He would end their relationship over this? Did her tardiness rule out all her other good qualities?

"I'd better go now." Arnie leaped out of his chair as if it had caught fire.

"Me, too." Dean jumped to his feet.

"Uh…happy birthday, Morgan." Arnie said, not meeting her gaze.

"Yeah, happy birthday," Dean parroted.

"Thank you," Morgan said as the two men fled.

"I guess I'd better go, too," Matt said with obvious reluctance. He glanced at Jack and grinned. "You've got your hands full. I'll catch you later."

***

Jack was scarcely aware of the room clearing out, of the quiet click of the front door closing. Morgan captured all his attention. Clearly she was fighting a raging internal battle. Her lips had parted, and she was breathing through her mouth, her chest heaving with each shuddering breath. Beneath the fabric of her ridiculously thin top, her nipples had formed hard points. Her hands were clenched into tight fists at her side. But her eyes betrayed her the most: widened by surprise, darkened to a deep blue by desire, they flashed with anger.

Her emotions mirrored his own. He was pissed off by her rudeness, hurt that she'd broken her promise, but turned on by the prospect of seeing her perfect, smooth and bare bottom turned over his knee in submission. Witnessing the evidence of her arousal stoked his desire even higher. His hardening cock throbbed. Would her pussy cream as he paddled her, he wondered?

Her disbelief that he would actually spank her strengthened his resolve to follow through. She had counted on her ability to wrap him around her little finger. And why not? It had worked in the past.

Not this time. He would spank her. Despite her promises, she'd arrived late, inconveniencing and embarrassing him and their guests. She wasn't aware of the party, but she had known he had been planning something special. And she hadn't cared enough to arrive home on time.

"Are you going to make it right?" His heart raced.

It was vitally important that Morgan capitulate. More was at stake than correcting her chronic tardiness. The nature of their relationship needed to change.

Her blue eyes filled with tears, intensifying the color. Her lower lip trembled. "I said I was sorry." Her hands twisted. "I promise I won't be late again. I know I said that before, but I'll try harder this time."

Jack's heart clenched. She looked like a little girl who'd lost her kitten. He longed to give in to her, kiss her and make it better, but he had to stand firm. Their relationship wouldn't survive if she could walk all over him.

He shook his head. "Not good enough, Babe. You have to prove it."

"By letting you spank me?"

He nodded. "You said you wouldn't be late, and I said there would be consequences if you were. We both have to stand by our word."

"Jack...please," she said.

"Enough, Morgan." He steeled himself against her pleading gaze. "Yes or no. What's your answer?"

Jack watched as Morgan bit her lip. Her gaze dropped to her feet. Silence hung heavy in the room.

"Yes," she responded in a small voice.

Relief and a white-hot spike of desire shot through him.

He strove to control signs of both. "Thank you, Morgan," he said in a measured tone. He pushed his chair back. "Come here." His heart jackhammered in his chest, and his cock was rock hard. His balls ached.

Morgan crept forward on leaden feet. It floored her that Jack was immune to her tears, that he was truly going to follow up on this threat. She'd acted angry, hurt, contrite, scared. None of it had worked. She'd even turned on the waterworks. He'd never been impervious to her tears before! She had apologized and promised to do better. What more could she do? How would a spanking solve the problem anyway?

What had gotten into him? He didn't have the right to treat her like a disobedient child, to punish her! Now, if he wanted to spank her for fun… That she could go along with eagerly.

Even knowing he was going to spank her for the wrong reasons, she was getting wet. Her tight nipples hurt. She wanted his hands on her naked bottom, but not like this. He was so calm, so smug. Like he was her boss or master or something.

She inched closer, and Jack's fingers closed around her wrist. His touch was warm, surprisingly gentle, as he pulled her over his lap. Her stomach contracted as she collided with the rock-hard evidence of his desire. Her pussy let down a surge of moisture. How could she feel humiliated and turned on at the same time?

Cool air caressed her bottom when he flipped up her short skirt, baring her ass, her lace thong offering little cover. Even that minute protection disappeared when he stripped off the minuscule panty and tossed it aside. She'd never felt more exposed and vulnerable.

The balance of power had shifted, and she didn't like it. She called the shots. Not Jack. But she couldn't ignore her body's response. She tingled from the roots of her highlighted hair to the tips of her freshly pedicured toes, and every part in between.

Morgan flinched as his palms smoothed over her ass. Almost lovingly, he caressed the soft, tender globes. She frowned in confusion. Maybe he wasn't going to spank her. The delicate strokes of his hands and the erection digging into the stomach seemed to indicate otherwise.

His hands cupped the moons of her ass, smoothing light circles, squeezing gently. Jack had always told her she had a nice ass and occasionally playfully smacked her tush, but he'd never paid it as much attention as he was now. Her butt tingled where his fingers trailed over her skin. Her skin felt hypersensitive, totally attuned to every caress as if it was the first time he'd ever touched her. Her pussy was growing wetter by the second. Her hips lifted a little, her legs parting slightly. She wiggled.

"Stop moving," he ordered.

"Please… J…AAACCK," she cried as his palm unexpectedly stung her cheek with a loud crack. Heat and pain radiated outward from the point of contact. A couple of seconds later the next spank fell on her other cheek, no less hard than the first. He took his time, spanking with careful deliberation and sharpness. The spanking was real and it stung. These were no playful smacks. Hot, angry tears welled in her eyes. All feelings of desire evaporated. There was nothing arousing or fun about this! After several searing swats, she covered her bottom with her hands.

"Move your hands, Morgan," he commanded.

"It hurts!" she protested.

"It's supposed to."

"You're mean! I said I was sorry. It's my birthday!"

"You always say you're sorry, but I don't think you mean it. If you did, you wouldn't keep doing it. Move your hands or you'll get another five swats." He spoke quietly, but with authority and determination.

She couldn't handle five more. She didn't know how she would endure thirty-three! She wouldn't be able to sit down for a week. She was seeing a whole new side of Jack. She wouldn't be able to deter him from this course of action. She could refuse to comply, of course, but that would mean risking the relationship. She wasn't ready to do that. Taking a deep breath, her hands moved to grip the legs of the chair.

Jack's palm came down hard. Sharp pain tore through her flesh in waves then mingled with a weird electric sensation. A shock of heated energy, almost sexual, sizzled at the point of contact and spiraled outward. Her clit tingled. Her eyes widened. Another sharp crack and pain merged with a pleasure that had her gasping in shock. With each strike, his stinging hand sensitized her nerve endings, reawakened her body's sexual demands. She became ultra aware of Jack's corded muscles contracting with every minuscule shift in position, felt the rough fabric of his pants chafing against her abdomen, heard his breathing quicken, smelled his heat and her own arousal. Her pussy was swelling, seeping with moisture. Her breasts, dangling over Jack's lap, felt heavy and full. Her nipples drew up into tight, aching beads.

"You will not...disrespect me...any more...Do you understand?" Jack punctuated each pause with a hard spank.

Morgan's emotions roiled. She was furious with Jack for his figurative and literal heavy-handedness. But her body craved his stinging touch; she was gripped in a lust so fierce she feared she would explode. She pressed her lips together, afraid if she opened her mouth, she'd howl in anger, scream in pleasure.

"What?" His hand struck her ass again.

"No! I mean Yes, Jack. Yes, I understand." Her senses verged on overload. Both sets of cheeks burned, her ass from the spanking and her face from anger and sexual arousal. "Please...Jack..."

"Please what?"

Please spank me more. Fuck me. The words threatened to spill out, but she wouldn't allow him the satisfaction. She couldn't help that she was aroused, but it wasn't right that he thought he had the authority to punish her. "Finish...get it over with." Was that pleading voice, really hers?

She felt him shake his head. "This is part of your lesson. We'll do things according to *my* timetable tonight."

She stifled a moan as his hands smoothed over her buttocks, easing the sting but ratcheting up her lust. She quivered. "Such a pretty pink," he murmured. "So pink and rosy and there's more to go."

Morgan shuddered as Jack's hand smacked her hard. He made her wait, allowing the painful pleasure of anticipation to build, for the sensation to sizzle through her before striking again. Morgan bit her lip, struggling to maintain a semblance of control over her growing lust. Her clit was burning, her pussy weeping, and a near-overpowering desire urged her to grind her pelvis against the hardness beneath her.

"Five more, Morgan." Jack was panting slightly.

She couldn't prevent a moan as the final spanks seared her flesh. At last, he eased her off his lap. She hastily adjusted her skirt to cover herself, wincing as her fingers brushed her inflamed, tender bottom. Her legs wobbled, and Jack gripped her elbow to steady her.

She glared at him, a storm of emotions swirling within her: fury, embarrassment, and a knee-weakening hunger. Her pussy was swollen, her inner thighs were wet with her moisture, and her beaded nipples were saluting through her shirt. She didn't know what made her madder—that he'd actually spanked her or that it aroused her like nothing ever had.

To calm her roiling thoughts, Morgan focused on the empty chairs where the men had been seated. She noticed absently that Matt's leather jacket was still draped over the chair. He'd forgotten it. Her gaze took in the empty room, the remains of the party she'd missed still in evidence. This was so not how she expected to celebrate her birthday—to be punished like a spoiled child. She was thirty years old! Humiliation and lust twisted together in tight knot. She swallowed the lump in her throat. She would not cry. She wouldn't give him the satisfaction. She lifted her chin.

A king on his throne, Jack leaned back in his chair. A triumphant smile played on his lips, and she itched to slap it off his face. Her gaze shifted to the near-empty bottle of beer.

It was full enough.

"Don't even think about dumping that over my head."

"I wasn't," Morgan denied, flushing hot. She was going to pour it in his lap!

He finished off the beer, and plunked the bottle on the table. "From now on, every time you make me cool my heels, I'm going to tan your backside."

Morgan tossed her head. "You and what army?" She winced at how juvenile and ridiculous she sounded. He'd just proven he didn't need an army. Chaos was making her head whirl. Warring physical sensations dueled with her bruised emotions. Her tender ass throbbed with pain, while the swollen flesh between her legs ached with need. She wanted to slap Jack's face, and she wanted to fuck him until she couldn't move. Underneath it all was a creeping sense of guilt that maybe she had been at fault. Jack was so accommodating, so easygoing that for him to have actually turned her over his knee and spanked her, he must have been pushed to the edge of his patience. Unable to process it all, she spun around and flounced away with as much pride as she could muster.

In the kitchen, she stopped short at the sight of the trays of half-eaten food and a big lopsided strawberry cake with cream cheese icing. "HAPPY…MOR" was scrawled in uneven letters on two lines, and Morgan surmised it had said "Happy Birthday Morgan" before the guests had eaten it. A pink heart made of icing decorated one corner of the cake.

From the look of it, Jack had baked the cake himself.

A magnum of unopened champagne chilled in a bucket, the ice turned to slush.

The impact of her actions seeped into her as she stared at the remains of the party.

Jack was right.

She was wrong.

She'd deliberately delayed coming home, reluctant to face Jack, but it had been inconsiderate to him and the guests who wanted to celebrate with her. She'd missed her own birthday party—a party Jack had worked hard to plan.

How many other events had they missed because of her tardiness? How often had Jack waited while she finished—or started—one more thing?

Jack was right. She had behaved like a self-centered, spoiled brat. No wonder he had spanked her. She had deserved it.

She hoped she could make it up to him. That he would let her.

She loved him to the depth of her being. Even mediocre sex wouldn't change that. Judging from his hard-on, Jack had enjoyed spanking her as much as she had enjoyed being spanked. If she could spice up their sex life by getting him to do it as foreplay instead of punishment…

***

Jack hesitated outside the kitchen door. The reddened palm of his hand still tingled. He could imagine how tender Morgan's ass felt. But if he could rewind the clock, he'd still spank her. He couldn't back down or she would never respect him. And how could she love him if she didn't respect him? But how could she love him after he'd publicly embarrassed her?

Jack rubbed his jaw. He'd threatened to spank her in front of his friends. They'd left so he could do it.

She'd been furious. But judging from the wet spot on his slacks, maybe, possibly, aroused?

The spanking had turned him on. Christ. He was still hard. Seeing her perfect bottom blush as pink as her pussy had turned his cock to stone. Her whimpers, which had sounded more like pleasure than protest, had made his balls ache. He glanced at the telltale spot on his pants leg.

That evidence fanned a flicker of hope that their sex life could be different. If he gradually introduced new things…

First he had to patch things up. If he could.

Raking a hand through his hair, Jack took a deep breath and pushed through the swinging kitchen door—cautiously, in case Morgan lobbed a frying pan at his head.

It wasn't a skillet that hit him, but Morgan's entire body

as she launched herself into his arms.

"Oh Jack, I'm so sorry!" Her arms wrapped tightly around his waist, her face burrowed into the crook of his neck. "I was wrong. Please forgive me."

Jack's heart thudded in relief, and he expelled his tension in a whoosh. His arms closed around her, and he settled his chin on the top of her head.

"I'm sorry, I'm sorry." Her words were muffled against his shirt.

"It's okay." His hands smoothed over her back to comfort her and to reassure himself that everything was okay between them. He was amazed she wasn't angry anymore.

Her soft breasts flattened against his chest, her pelvis pressed against his. She looked up at him. Tears glistened in her eyes. "I promise I'll never be late again. I've said that before, but I'll prove it to you."

His chest tightened. He believed her this time. He could read the sincerity, true remorse in her gaze, her tone. "Ah, Morgan—" He could feel the heat radiating off her, as he slipped his hands under her short skirt and cupped her ass cheeks. He replayed the picture of her curvy ass turning rosy. His grip tightened.

Morgan moaned.

"Christ! I'm sorry." His touch gentled. Of course, she was sore. He'd spanked her, for God's sake.

"No," she said, "You're not hurting me. At least…not in a bad way."

"I needed to shake you up. You weren't getting it and …"

"Don't apologize." She shook her head. "I'm the one who should be sorry. And I am. You were right."

Jack hugged her. He wanted to laugh in relief and amazement at her change of heart. If he'd known that a little domestic discipline could make such a big difference in her attitude he might have spanked her a long time ago. He believed her remorse was sincere, but if tardiness became a problem in the future, he wouldn't hesitate to administer another spanking. But he would keep his intentions private. She was entitled to privacy.

Morgan buried her face against his chest. He felt her take a deep breath. "Jack?" her muffled voice sounded unsure, unlike the confident Morgan he knew.

"Yes?"

She raised her head. Her teeth worried her bottom lip. "Would you…would you…spank me again sometime, for fun instead of punishment?"

His jaw dropped. He couldn't have been more stunned if she'd socked him the chest. His heart skidded to a stop.

She misread his silence, and her face flushed crimson. She tried to pull away. "I'm sorry. Forget I said that."

He hung onto her, refusing to release her. Raw, sharp lust rocketed through him. "Oh God, Morgan."

Her head bowed; she wouldn't meet his gaze. "I'm a pervert."

He lifted her chin with his finger. "I must be one, too, because my cock's ready to explode."

"What?" She stared.

"Spanking you turned me on, too. Couldn't you tell how hard I was?"

She nodded. "Yes, but I still thought the purpose was to discipline me for being late."

"It was." He nodded. "But I hadn't realized how sexy it would be."

She giggled. "I think we scared Arnie and Dean."

Jack chuckled. "Yeah, they couldn't leave fast enough."

"Matt didn't seem to mind," she commented.

Jack hesitated before responding. She didn't know the half of it. In the old days—his randy, single days—he and Matt sometimes used to share women. His friend still did, and a while back had proposed a ménage with Morgan or a foursome with him and his girlfriend Janine. At the time, Jack was certain Morgan wouldn't go for it and told him so. He'd been equally certain just revealing Matt's invitation would send Morgan screaming into the night—and not in a good way—so he'd never told her. But now? Now, he realized Morgan was more woman than he'd ever thought she was. But he still couldn't predict how she would react.

"He wanted to participate." Jack paused, watching as surprise, then heat ignited in Morgan's eyes. "He wants to fuck you."

Morgan's lips formed an "oh."

"Does that shock you?" Jack eyed her. "To know that another man wants you?"

Slowly she shook her head. "It excites me," she said in a low voice.

Jack exhaled, still hesitant to pursue the conversation. That Morgan enjoyed knowing another man desired her was a typically feminine response. But it fell short of wanting to be fucked by another man or being willing to participate in a ménage.

He loved the pleasure teaming up brought women. But most women didn't go for it, and a couple of girlfriends, women he'd cared about, had broken up with him after he'd suggested it. The mere mention of the idea carried enormous risk. That was why he'd been reluctant to approach Morgan.

Jack's heart thudded. He traced Morgan's lips with his thumb. He held her gaze. "Do you want to fuck other men?"

Her lips parted. "I love you."

"I love you, too, but that's not the question."

She disengaged from his embrace. Her head dipped, her hair hiding her face. Jack's stomach plummeted, but he refused to let her turn away. They'd wasted so much time not communicating with each other. He tucked her hair behind her ear so he could see her face. She lifted her chin and met his gaze. "Sometimes… yes," she admitted.

Jack swallowed. He'd never imagined having this conversation with Morgan. But he'd never envisioned she would enjoy a little domestic discipline either. That she eagerly embraced being spanked emboldened him. He took a deep breath and plunged. "I want to watch you fuck another man. I want to do a threesome with you. I want to take turns fucking your hot, wet, tight pussy, then take you sandwich style."

Morgan trembled. Her braless breasts heaved, her nipples jutting out through her thin top. "Oh God," she moaned. "Jack…that's what I want. I love making love, but sometimes I need to be fucked."

His cock threatened to burst through his pants. "Do you want that now?"

"More than ever." She nodded.

"Take off your clothes," he growled.

She shucked her white top, baring her perfect cherry-tipped breasts, and slid her skirt down her legs.

Jack inhaled sharply. "What did you do?" He stared at her muff, totally bare, except for a small heart of fuzz.

"I had my pussy waxed at the spa. Do you like it?" She smiled coquettishly and stroked the small heart.

"Too much. If I hadn't already spanked you, I'd paddle your ass for sure."

Jack tore off his clothes, freeing his aching erection. He needed so much to fuck Morgan; once would not be enough. But he had all night. And he planned to use every second.

His gaze captured hers as he approached her. Her head tilted, and he covered her mouth with his. Desire, too long denied, exploded. He didn't coax or seduce, but commanded, his teeth nipping, his tongue lashing. Morgan whimpered, giving as good as she got.

His hands kneaded the smooth skin of her breasts. He tugged and pinched her nipples before capturing the tips in his mouth. He sucked fiercely the way she liked.

"So good, so good." She whimpered.

His tongue laved a bud, soothing any residual pain, then his teeth clamped onto her nipple and tugged anew.

Jack's hand trailed over her smooth, hot skin, pausing to tug on her belly button ring before journeying to her mound. He toyed with the fuzzy heart before dipping into her cleft.

Her folds had blossomed and swelled, and without the cover of hair, were as soft as dew-coated rose petals. He zeroed in on her clit, engorged with desire, and stroked it. Morgan's head fell back, her eyes squeezed shut, and she gasped.

He released her nipple to watch her face as he caressed her pussy. He slid two fingers into her tight depths, and groaned. Her vise-like cunt was as slick as liquid silk.

'I'm going to fuck you, Morgan," he growled. "I'm going to fuck you in ways you've only fantasized. Are you ready?"

Her eyes flew open. "Yes."

Jack slid a third finger into her. His gaze held hers. His heart pounded. "Should I call Matt? Have him come back?"

He watched as she wet her lips, swallowed. "Yes."

"I'm already here," came his buddy's voice and Morgan's cunt contracted around his fingers.

***

Morgan would have crumpled to the floor if Jack hadn't been supporting her. Matt leaned against the door jam, wearing a carnal grin and a leather jacket slung over his shoulder. His gaze locked onto her. She should have been embarrassed, horrified by Matt's presence, but instead sharp desire slammed through her, rocketing her to the top of the world.

With brazen exhibitionism, her back arched, and her legs parted wider as Jack's fingers picked up force and speed. Her clit throbbed and she cried out as a wave of ecstasy crashed over her. She called out Jack's name as she was swept away in a tsunami of sensation.

She crumpled then, collapsing into Jack's strong arms, her body trembling in the wake of the orgasm, reeling from the magnitude. The taboo act of being watched had heightened the experience, taken it to a whole new level of sensuality. Jack soothed her with stroking hands, smoothing the hair from her face, caressing her back and tender buttocks. His erection throbbed against her abdomen. His hands shook as he stroked her; he'd put his own needs on hold to pleasure her. His selflessness and caring suffused her with warmth. How could she ever have thought he was too nice?

"I thought you went home," Jack said to Matt.

"I forgot my jacket. I came back for it and heard my name."

She glanced from Matt to Jack, reading the lust in their faces. The same sexual longing gripped her. She'd experienced the best climax of her life, but she wanted more. Her gaze fixed on Jack, her needs too overwhelming to articulate.

But she didn't have to.

Jack's lips pressed to her ear. "This is for you, Sweetheart," he said in a low, throaty voice. "Matt and I are going to pleasure you all night. In all ways. Are you ready?"

She wet her lips. "More than you know." She wanted to pinch herself to ensure she wasn't dreaming. All the time she had longed for a more exciting sex life, Jack had wanted the same. Now he was offering her a chance to experience her deepest, most secret desire. She was so excited she thought she might burst.

A sly, sexy, heart-stopping grin lit Jack's face. He scooped her into his arms and carried her to the bedroom. Morgan peeked over his broad, muscled shoulder to see Matt flipping out his cell phone. It struck her as odd, but she wasn't going to focus on that. She buried her hot face in Jack's neck.

She trembled with the force of her needs, in anticipation. Tonight would open a new chapter in her relationship with Jack. Her rational mind urged her to consider the consequences, but she shushed it. Now wasn't the time to think, to chart a list of the pros and cons. Every fantasy, every desperate yearning was about to come true. Now was the time to experience, to feel.

She'd face reality in the morning. Hindsight was always clearer than foresight anyway.

Jack set her gently beside the bed. He kissed her and she surrendered to the pleasure of his touch. When she opened her eyes, Matt had entered the room and was divesting himself of his clothing. Lewd interest had her stomach quickening. Matt's nipples were pierced by golden rings. In contrast to his thick head of hair and his rough jaw, his muscled, toned body was shaved of body hair.

All his body hair, she realized, when his blue briefs hit the floor. Matt's cock wasn't quite as big as Jack's massive specimen, but he had more than enough to do the job, and the absence of pubic hair made him appear bigger. The crown was huge, the veined shaft thick and long. He had a fiercely masculine member and she wanted it. All of it. And Jack's. Her mouth went dry at the thought of having two men pleasure her.

Hands on her shoulders, Jack guided her to perch on the bed. He parted her thighs wide. She relished being on display, having two handsome, endowed, aroused men eye her as if she were a work of art. "Is this the prettiest pussy you've ever seen?" Jack asked Matt. "She got herself waxed today."

"She's sweet, all right. I love a bare cunt."

Their lewd comments sent desire skipping through her, and her pussy flooded with moisture, her breasts grew heavy, her nipples hardened.

Jack knelt between her spread legs. "I need to taste her." His head dipped, but she felt only the caress of his warm breath, little puffs of air that had her trembling for a more tangible touch. Her hands grabbed his head and tried to pull his face against her, but he resisted, brushing her inner thighs, her swollen folds, the hood of her clit, with a feather-light touch of his lips.

"Jack…don't tease me. " She pounded on his shoulders.

Matt moved bedside. "She's wild, isn't she?" The veins in his erect member pulsed, its head gleaming with pearly essence. Morgan's mouth watered.

"I'm going to make her wilder." The tip of Jack's wet tongue flicked over the hood of her clit, and Morgan's hips came off the bed.

"I'm assuming you have condoms so I can suit up?" Matt asked.

Jack pulled back and lightly stroked her with his fingers. "Top drawer of the nightstand. And hand me the anal lube."

They had anal lube? Since when? They had wasted so much time by not talking to each other. She wanted to smack him again, but he slid two fingers into her wet channel, and all she could focus on was the sensation zinging through her.

Matt extracted the box of condoms and set it on the nightstand. He handed Jack a tube. "Here you go."

Jack set the lube on the bed. "Thanks." His fingers continued to explore her, and she could feel her moisture pooling, running into the crack of her ass. At this rate, she wondered if she'd even need the lube.

Matt ran his hands over her breasts, tweaking her rosebud nipples, satisfaction etching his features as the hard buds pebbled further. "She has pretty tits," he said. His casual, carnal compliment filled her with warmth even as she was struck by the strangeness of him speaking about her rather than to her.

"Why are you talking to each other as if I'm not..... heeeeere," her protest ended on a moan, pleasure knifing through her, as Jack's mouth came down on her sex. Without the barrier of hair, the sensation was sharper. Or maybe it was because she was so turned on. Or because another man was watching. Or a combination of all three.

Jack's fingers peeled back her clitoral hood and opened her folds, then he licked her from cunt to clit. Her pussy contracted and the bundle of nerves at her core pulsed. She sucked in her breath as her desire turned molten.

Matt bent and drew her nipple into his mouth. The combination of his gentle tongue, his insistent lips and the abrasion of his unshaven jaw sent tingles racing through her. The taboo of having two men loving her had her senses and emotions reeling. The forbidden carnality electrified her. She was spinning on an adults-only amusement park ride, her inhibitions falling away as she whirled in wild circles.

Her sex was in flames. Jack's mouth was devouring her whole, lashing at her clit, lapping at her cream, nibbling on her swollen labia. And while his busy mouth was driving her wild, his fingers were unscrewing the cap from the tube of lube. Her stomach quickened in anticipation. She'd craved this, dreamt about it, fantasized, yearned; she couldn't believe it was finally happening. She and Jack were finally on the same page.

Her view of Jack was blocked as Matt released her nipple, rose and pressed his throbbing cock to her lips. "Suck me, Morgan."

Hungrily, she complied. He tasted creamy and salty, his crown as smooth as an ice cream cone, but warm and much better. He wasn't quite as large as Jack, but that only made him easier to accommodate in her mouth. It felt strange, foreign to suck a cock other than Jack's but exciting also, the thrill heightened by Jack watching, encouraging.

Relaxing her muscles, she took Matt deep into her throat, fitting as much of his shaft in her mouth as she could. Her hands encircled the base of his rod, working him with a firm grip as she sucked him.

Matt swore and began to thrust. "Christ Jack, she's going to suck my 'nads out through my dick." His guttural curse drove a stab of pleasure into her core.

His fingers, tangled in her hair, held her captive, but she was a willing hostage to the lust coursing through her. She'd never felt such raw, sexual excitement. It was primitive, wild, and growing stronger by the second.

Jack increased suction on her clit as Matt fucked her mouth, and her own hips moved of their own accord. Pressure built between her legs, and she knew she was close to coming. Her womb ached with anticipation when Jack applied cool lube to the ring of her anus and pressed a finger inside her. Her tight portal resisted with a twinge, but then accepted the penetration greedily. Molten delight coursed through her. As he sucked hard on her inflamed clit, he slowly finger-fucked her ass. Intoxicated, she reveled in the delicious pressure, the building tension. This is what she'd longed for, this wild, all-encompassing carnal expression that stoked and fed her hunger simultaneously. Gratitude, joy and lust welled up inside in a churning conflagration of emotion. Her mouth tightened around Matt's cock, sucking him hard as shudders wracked her body. Her senses were inflamed by the rapturous joy of having two men to pleasure her receptive, responsive body.

When a second finger joined the first in her anal channel, she lost it. Fire coalesced into a burning knot and then exploded. Her body was a star of contracting and expanding sensation. Her clit and her pussy contracted almost painfully as the second orgasm of the evening rocketed through her. She would have screamed, but Matt's cock muffled her shriek of pleasure.

Jack's fingers and mouth worked her until her tremors subsided. "I can't wait anymore. I need to fuck her now," he growled to Matt. His thick tone, heated words renewed the tingles of sexual delight racing through her. She ached for him to be as excited by the threesome as she was.

"Fuck! Hurry up." Matt pulled out of her mouth and knelt on the bed.

Jack flipped her onto her hands and knees. "Suck Matt's cock while I fuck your pussy." He sharply slapped her tender ass. A savage, primal gratification swelled at his rough tone and manner. Her clit was still pulsing, little contractions rippling though her cunt from the orgasm. Eagerly, she crawled to Matt. She licked his cockhead, her tongue flicking over the opening, tracing the ridge. He thrust his hips forward, but she retreated, teasing him. The bed depressed, and she peered back to see Jack preparing to mount her. Her breath caught in her throat. Jack had a massive erection normally, but now he appeared even longer, thicker, the skin stretched taut. The huge plum of a crown glistened.

She sucked Matt's cock into her mouth, her lips closing tight. Matt's fingers captured her nipples, tugging on the distended tips, squeezing, pinching, whipping her arousal to a savage frenzy. His touch felt so different from Jack's, but no less devastating.

Jack's fingers were spreading her open. The massive head of his cock probed her creaming core, then he plunged, driving his rod balls-deep into her, propelling her forward, to take Matt's cock deep. She was rocked between two hard cocks and the sensation made her senses reel. She was on a roller coaster ride of whirling, rapturous sensation. For the first time in her relationship with Jack, she felt free to act with abandon, to express her sexuality totally.

Jack didn't ask like he usually did, "Is this okay, is this too hard?" but fucked her forcefully and fast. This is what she'd been needing all along: a man who got it. A man who didn't ask permission, who didn't tiptoe around her. A man who instinctively knew how to fill her needs.

Jack manipulated her clit with one hand, tormenting the sensitive bud, hurling her into a spiral of wanton lust. His other hand returned to her anus, stretching the opening with his fingers.

Matt's pace matched Jack's. His fingers manipulated her nipples fiercely, pinching and twisting, sending shafts of painful pleasure into the core of her. She loved a firm, very firm, touch on her nipples, and Matt was doing it just right.

She reveled in the completeness of their possession: a cock in her cunt, one in her mouth; fingers on her clit, in her ass, twisting her nipples. Her besieged body was under their control, and she could do little but hang on for the ride, but oh, what a ride it was. The men worked in tandem, the thrusts of each one driving her to take the other deeper. They filled her body and fed the hunger that had ached inside her for so long.

The fiery tension was building to a fever pitch in her clit when Matt's control snapped. He let loose with a harsh growl and pumped his essence into her hungry mouth. She moaned in delight with her creamy treat but then gasped as Jack slapped—slapped!—her exposed, sensitized clit.

Stinging sensation shot through the tiny organ and rippled though her body. It was agonizing, painfully pleasurable. She wanted to tell him to stop; she wanted to beg for more, but her mouth was filled with cock and come. Everything she thought she'd known about making love shattered, and she soared to uncharted heights of ecstasy. She marveled at the masterful, bold Jack who had a new bag of sexual tricks to drive her to unbearable bliss.

Jack slapped her again, several sharp, short smacks. "Come, Morgan, now!" Jack ordered through gritted teeth.

Her body responded obediently to his command, igniting her clit in a burst of orgasmic fire. Her cunt convulsed, milking Jack's cock, and he shouted her name as his own climax swept over him, and his spasming cock filled her with his hot seed.

Jack slumped over her, his strong arms taking his weight. His breath blew hot against her skin. He kissed her neck, caressing her with his lips, and Morgan tilted her head to the side.

"Oh, my God, Jack." She was flooded with such overpowering emotion she didn't know whether to laugh or cry. It wasn't just the earth-shattering orgasm that left her shell-shocked. It was this new masterful side of Jack: the one who commanded instead of followed, who took instead of asked, who made her feel more sexy than she'd ever felt in her life. Who seemed to share her carnal desires. Who was willing to share her to satisfy her.

Jack's lips brushed her ear. "That was just the appetizer," he whispered wickedly before nipping her neck. Pleasure shot through her at his heated promise and stinging touch.

Jack stretched out, pulling her onto her side, facing him. Matt curved his muscled body around her backside. Jack kissed her lazily, but thoroughly, exploring her with his tongue. Then Matt tugged her gently toward him and covered her mouth with his. Together they took turns rolling her between them, kissing her unhurriedly. Hands and fingers caressed her with feather light strokes, managing to be everywhere—in her hair, on her breasts and butt cheeks, between her legs. She felt cherished, sexy, like she was the most adored woman in the world. Gentle fingers filled her pussy, slipped into her ass, worked more cream inside her.

"You're so snug, Morgan. You're going to fit like a glove."

Jack's voice rumbled in her ear.

"Mmmm," she mumbled in agreement, the sound muffled by Matt's kiss.

She surrendered to them, floating on bliss, scarcely aware of what they were doing, only that it felt so good. Tempered for the moment was the blazing lust, but it was no less erotic to be petted so leisurely. Desire ignited in the pit of her stomach. Her pussy flooded with wet warmth and the tender peaks of her breasts began to harden.

The smell of sex, of her aroused pussy, of Jack's seed, of their combined male musk, infused her senses with heady aroma. It was the scent of desire and fulfillment, of fantasy realized. She wanted to absorb the fragrance into her skin, bathe herself in the essence.

Gradually their desultory caresses became more passionate. She found herself stretched out on her back. Jack captured a turgid nipple between his lips and Matt did likewise, their gentle laving turning to a sweet, pleasurably painful suction. She arched in erotic abandon, jutting out her swollen breasts, swimming with rapture at having both breasts tended to.

She grasped a cock in each hand, her fingers unable to meet around the thick shafts. They felt hot and impossibility hard, warmed steel rods against her palms. Her hands moved over them, stroking, squeezing, wanting to give them the same pleasure that rushed through her.

Matt's hand slipped between her thighs and he groaned. "Sweet," he growled. His touch was different from Jack's but the strangeness of it heightened her desire, and her legs splayed wide. Her gaze sought Jack's, and his smile of approval and satisfaction made her heart swell with adoration and confidence. She surrendered to Matt's expert fingers, which homed in on her clit, stroking the bud, first delicately, and then with greater pressure and speed. Twice he brought her to the brink of orgasm, only to pull her back from the edge.

"Matt, please," she arched, thrashing after the second near miss. "Let me come."

"Not yet, Morgan," Matt said. "You're not quite ready."

Not ready? She was creaming, orgasm only a flick away. She frowned in confusion. Her head whirled, making it difficult to grasp concrete thoughts. She floated in a haze of erotic abandon.

Matt and Jack switched position so she was cradled between Matt's thighs, her own legs spread wide. Behind her, Matt's hard, shaven body felt like a plank of polished steel, his cock a piston digging into her back. Jack stretched out, watching as his buddy continued to stroke her. Sharp piercing desire stabbed through her at the passionate, primal satisfaction etched on Jack's face. Morgan didn't think she'd ever experienced anything as erotic as this moment.

"Bring her close, one more time," Jack said. "Don't let her go over."

Matt's fingers trailed over her belly to her core, teasing, no, tormenting her. He circled and stroked her clit until she was writhing. Then, after a nod from Jack, he lifted her thighs and planted her knees to her chest, exposing her cunt and ass.

"Jack…Matt." Her head thrashed with her need for release. She'd never realized she was capable of such intense desire. Or maybe she did. Perhaps her body, her soul had known all along.

Jack grabbed the tube of anal lubricant and liberally applied it to his erection. Her eyes widened as she realized he intended to fuck her in the ass in the missionary position. She'd never done it that way before. Nor had she ever had her back entrance reamed by a man as large as Jack. Her heart fluttered and she swallowed hard. Could she take him? She had to. Her body and soul demanded it. She needed to know that they could fulfill each other's sexual needs.

"I want to watch your face as I fuck you," Jack said. "When I tell you, bear down."

"Okay." Her voice was a squeak. Liquid heat pooled between her legs. Trepidation quickened in her stomach, but it was desire that dominated her senses, that had her puckered rear entrance contracting in anticipation.

"It's going to hurt a little at first, but the pleasure will come, I promise."

"Okay."

Jack leaned forward and captured her lips in a soft kiss. His lips caressed, his tongue stroked. His own masculine flavor, the hint of cigar, and the vestiges of her own tang combined in a heady concoction. Under his gentle touch, her uneasiness melted away. She loved Jack. She trusted him.

He lifted his head and peered into her eyes. "If you need me to stop, say tulips. Okay?"

"Tulips. But, I won't. Just fuck me, Jack," she said.

He grinned. "With pleasure, Sweetheart."

Jack guided his cock to her tightly closed portal. He was huge against her, and new doubts arose about his size. What if he didn't fit? His hips shifted, and he pressed firmly against her. "Now, Morgan," he ordered.

She bore down, relaxing her muscles, and he pushed hard. Her reluctant sphincter held fast at first, but then surrendered to the greater force, and the enormous knob of his cock surged into her, shooting flames up her ass.

Tulips! Tulips! Her mind cried out, but she bit back the words. Her mouth opened in a silent gasp, the air caught in her lungs, and stars danced behind her eyes. Her hands fisted in the bedcovers. She was swamped by sensations of carnal hunger, searing heat, wanton joy, and a curiously satisfying pain. The intimacy of it made her want to weep. In this moment they were one. But could her body handle it?

"You're big." Her voice was a breathy squeak.

"You can take me, Sweetheart. The hard part is over. Just breathe, Morgan. Take a breath, Sweetheart."

His soothing voice eliminated all vestiges of anxiety. She expelled the air she'd been holding and panted, overriding her protesting muscles. Beneath the burn existed a raw need that could only be fulfilled in this way. She bore down again and pushed against him. "More, Jack. Give me more. All of you."

Her eyes locked on Jack's as he rocked slowly but firmly,

working his erection inch by huge inch into her until he was buried balls-deep inside her. The intimacy of his possession, his desire to make it good for her made her feel as if she would burst with love for him. It wasn't only her body's desires that were being fulfilled but her heart's as well.

"You're so beautiful, Morgan." Jack's eyes blazed passion and approval.

She had a cock the size of a small bat inside her body. She'd never been filled so full. Her pussy could never accommodate the entire length of his cock. Her anal channel did. Her tissues still burned, but her clit began to pulse with need and her womb contracted hungrily. As desire swelled, pain receded, leaving in its wake an exquisite, awesome pressure, a yearning for more. Her anal muscles clenched in pleasure. She'd never felt closer to Jack than she did at this moment. Her need, her love for him was elemental, primitive, all-encompassing.

"Get her vibrator. It's in the nightstand," Jack spoke to Matt.

As Matt slipped out from behind her, allowing her to lie flat against the bed, Jack lifted her legs over his shoulders and drove his cock deeper. Slowly, excruciatingly slowly, he fucked her. His expression rapt, he focused on their merging bodies. Morgan wished, she, too could see his cock rocking in her ass, her body opening, accepting him.

But what she couldn't see, she could feel. She was stretched beyond the limits she'd thought possible, and he was stroking her from the inside out. The pain evaporated into fuzzy memory, and only a piercing pleasure remained, a pleasure even more shattering. Nothing in her imagination had prepared her for the rapture of his possession. She desperately hoped this would be a new beginning in their relationship.

A buzzing filled Morgan's ears, and then Matt appeared with her vibrator. He stroked it over her body, her nipples, her lower abdomen, before touching her clit. As Matt teased her with the toy, he worked the hard buds of her breasts with lips and teeth. A delicious agonizing tension was building, a yearning alternately fed and denied by the cock burrowing inside her, the teasing application of the vibrator, the nips and tugs of Matt's mouth on her aching nipples. Desire flowed thickly through her veins. Her head thrashed with the excruciating need for ultimate completion.

She craved it hard. Fast. Rough. Her hands twisted in Matt's hair. Her heels hooked on Jack's shoulders, her hips thrusting, driving him deeper. The more he gave, the more she wanted.

"Oh God, fuck me harder, Jack. Harder."

Jack drove into her as Matt tugged her nipple with his teeth. He worked the vibrator on her clit catching the bud on fire. A savage urge drove her to spiral higher and higher until her body climaxed in waves of sensation. Her clit and cunt convulsed painfully, her rectum contracting forcefully, squeezing Jack's cock.

"Fuck, Morgan. Fuck. Fuck. Fuck." Jack's control snapped and he pounded into her. She loved the sound of his hard, involuntary cry as much as she relished his possession. It infused her with a sense of feminine power and humbleness to know she had driven him to brink of control, that he was as desperate for her as she was for him. She could feel his seed shooting deep, and she clenched her muscles as tight as she could, milking him for all she was worth.

Her orgasm had barely subsided when Jack pulled out, and Matt rolled on a condom. Her stomach fluttered. Everything she'd already done had taken her on a new path in her relationship with Jack, but allowing Matt to fuck her would be tantamount to leaping off a cliff. What would happen when she landed at the bottom? Would Jack still be there? Suddenly she needed reassurance. Her eyes sought Jack's. His gaze blazed with approval, desire, and masculine satisfaction, and her heart gave a hitch of relief.

Matt mounted her, his cock probing her slick vaginal opening.

Morgan reached out to Jack, and he clasped her hand, squeezing her fingers. "You're so beautiful. So hot," he said.

Matt's hips lifted and with one plunge he drove into her cunt. The suddenness of it, the size of him, had her crying out, but it was so good, so fucking good. If not for Jack's massive cock, she would have said Matt had the biggest cock she'd ever seen, certainly ever had inside her.

"Holy fuck she's tight," Matt swore. "Like a goddamn virgin."

"Wait 'til you try her ass," Jack said.

"Next round," Matt said.

Next round? She didn't have time to ponder that because Matt was pumping now, hard and deep, his pistoning shaft rubbing her clit, igniting fiery sensations. She hung onto the lifeline of Jack's hand and surrendered to the feeling, meeting Matt's thrusts with her own. Her hard nipples ached for attention. Jack must have read her mind because he seized one taut bud in his mouth and lashed it with his tongue, scraping his teeth across the sensitized flesh. She was in heaven, her body in a state of bliss from wild, relentless fucking, her heart swelling with rapture and gratitude.

Jack bit into her, and she couldn't hold it anymore. She came in a supernova blast of sensation that had her hips bucking, her womb and cunt spasming, her hand nearly crushing Jack's fingers.

Matt uttered a guttural cry and convulsed inside her, his body releasing.

Morgan lay spent as the two men disappeared into the bathroom. Her mind couldn't wrap itself around what was happening. Before Jack, she'd participated in some wild sex, but never had her lovers taken such care to tend to her needs as Jack and Matt had. Jack had been so voracious, so commanding, so attentive. Everything she'd believed to be true about him and their relationship was shattering like crystal falling on granite. She didn't know what to believe anymore. The foundation she'd thought was firm beneath her was shifting like sand. Was any of this even real?

As she'd fucked his best friend, Jack had watched with such

satisfaction and obvious enjoyment, it made her heart sing. But in the fading sex-infused glow, doubt hummed a familiar haunting melody. Her first love, her high school boyfriend, had literally and figuratively popped both her cherries, taking her virginity and initiating her into the joy of anal sex, but then he'd married a girl from his parent's church. A virgin, who no doubt, refused to let him anywhere near her back entrance.

Another lover, an attorney at a big name law firm, introduced her to ménage but as his career heated up, his passion cooled.

"You're a great girl, Morgan. I love the way you love sex. You'll always be special to me, but I'm hoping to make partner. I have to think about my career and word gets, out, you know?"

It had become a theme in her life. Lovers enjoyed her, then dumped her for someone less…enjoyable. She was great to play with, but they didn't want to grow old with her.

Then she'd met Jack. Decent. Nice. Sexually-conservative Jack.

Just what she needed.

Almost.

She didn't want to fuck madly all the time. Not even most of the time. But sometimes? Yes, sometimes she craved it.

And now Jack had revealed a wild side. She had a strong hunch he'd participated in other ménages. Judging from how he and Matt communicated and fucked with such coordination, she suspected they'd teamed up before.

Morgan stretched, arching her back. Jack was filling all her desires, making her fantasies real. Her reservations about a future with him evaporated like a wisp in the sun.

But how did he feel?

Would the threesome destroy his feelings for her? Would the old double standard rear its ugly head? It was ironic, that less than half a day ago her biggest fear was that Jack wanted to marry her. Now, she was afraid he wouldn't think she was wife material.

She wanted him more, now. Not less.

What would she do if he didn't feel the same way? How would she bear it?

The men returned from the bathroom and Morgan sucked in her breath. Both were tall, muscled with washboard abs and bulging biceps, and Christ, were they hung. While Matt was slightly taller, had slightly larger muscles, Jack was more handsome and won out in the endowment department, although Matt was no slouch.

They knelt beside her, and with moist cloths, proceeded to clean her from head to toe, wiping away the perspiration and come. They were especially meticulous and gentle in cleaning between her legs and the cheeks of her ass. The washcloths disappeared, and their hands and mouths followed the path of the cleaning, exploring her body languidly, thoroughly. Morgan sighed in contentment, letting her uncertainties fall away.

Jack kissed her, lightly but possessively, his mouth moving on her swollen, tender lips. She arched into him, sucking on his tongue, feeding on his strength and tenderness. His lips trailed over her skin to her ear, her neck, her shoulders. His mouth found her navel, and his teeth tugged on her belly button ring before traveling to her breasts and then back to her lips. She got the impression he meant to love her with his body, and warmth pooled within her. Surely he wouldn't treat her so adorningly if his feelings had changed?

She tried to cling to that thought, but it slipped away as Matt parted her legs, wedging his wide shoulders between her thighs. His thumbs opened her folds and then his mouth was upon her, growling in satisfaction, licking as if she were a banquet, and he had all the time in the world to enjoy her. The butterfly strokes of his lips and tongue were offset by the scrape of his unshaven jaw, rasping erotically at her most delicate flesh. She would be chafed from his beard, but the glorious sensation was worth the price. Her hips lifted, begging for more. She was enveloped in blissful haze where the only thing that mattered were the intoxicating sensations humming through her.

Matt penetrated her pussy with two fingers and slid his thumb into her ass. Her muscles clenched. Her body began to thrust as the tension grew tighter and tighter. Her body had been finely tuned by their lovemaking, and she was speeding toward orgasm.

"She's going to blow. I need to fuck her," Matt growled.

"Do it," Jack said.

She glanced in confusion from one man to the other as Jack stretched out on his back and pulled her atop him.

"But Matt…" she protested, not understanding. Wasn't Matt going to fuck her?

"Ride my cock, Morgan," Jack ordered and her disappointment evaporated.

Obediently she impaled herself on his erection. She sighed in pleasure as his huge tool stretched her pussy. She wanted to rock, seek a rhythm, but Jack's muscled arms clamped her to his chest. She heard, rather than saw, Matt donning a condom.

The bed depressed.

A lubed cock – Matt's cock – probed her rear.

Her breath caught in her throat. Nervousness and lust twisted in her stomach.

Then came pressure. Intense pressure. Her body opened and he surged inside. Flames ignited at the entry. A mewing sound erupted from her throat as he filled, overfilled her anal channel, made tighter by the double penetration. She tried to scream Jack's name, but couldn't find her voice.

"Jesus Christ!" Matt swore.

He tunneled deep, burning his way in. Pleasure – pain – she couldn't differentiate which was which. With a cock in her pussy and one in her rectum, she was stuffed to capacity, her delicate tissues stretched to the max. She didn't think she could take any more. She could feel their cocks pulsating. The world outside her body ceased to exist. Captured between two men, her mind, body and soul were reduced to raw, primitive sensation. The scent of sex, raw and earthy, invaded her nostrils. Harsh breathing, hers and theirs, filled her ears. Rational thought evaporated, and there was nothing left but gnawing hunger.

A driving need urged her hips to move, but she was pinned between hard male bodies. She whimpered, unable to articulate what she needed. "Oh, God, Jack…it's too…I need…help me…"

"Ssh, Honey. We're going to take it easy…at first." Jack kissed her and she drew from his strength.

Matt shifted and began to pump inside her, a slow slide that both eased and stoked her churning, wanton needs. When Jack picked up the rhythm in her cunt, she thought she was going to lose her mind from the savage, unbearable ecstasy. Her two lovers fucked in tandem, like a well-oiled machine, sliding in and out of her, awakening sensations of a magnitude she'd never experienced.

The angle of their thrusts placed direct contact on her engorged clit and caused her hard nipples to scrape against the coarse hair on Jack's chest. Her buttocks, tender from the spanking she'd received, registered every lunge of Matt's pelvis. Her lungs couldn't suck enough air and she panted, her gasps echoed by the heavy breathing of Jack and Matt. Their hearts hammered against her, the beats matching her own rapid rhythm. Desperate, she kissed Jack, devouring him with her mouth, biting his lips, his neck, his shoulders. She was a cat in heat, howling, fighting for ultimate completion. Jack was her mate, her lover, her life, and he was giving her this ultimate carnal experience.

As if on cue, their pace quickened, their thrusts turned rougher, deeper, faster, transmitting ripples of delight that shuddered through her swollen, creaming cunt, her tight anal muscles. The pressure ballooned. Jack seized her nipples, twisting the reddened buds. Excruciating pleasure cascaded from her nipples to her womb. They were killing her with pleasure.

"Oh god oh god harder god harder fuck me harder," she

begged in a reedy voice.

"Yes, baby. Take us, Morgan. Take us. That's it, baby, take it," Jack growled his praise.

Their cocks pounded into her, and she convulsed in a full-body orgasm, every muscle contracting, every nerve ending burning white-hot.

"Jack!" Over and over she screamed his name.

Groaning, he came then, his cock shuddering violently, shooting spunk deep into her womb. A millisecond later, Matt's teeth latched onto the back of her neck as his rod jerked in her ass, rocked by his own orgasm.

***

Morgan lost count of the orgasms that tore through her, as Jack and Matt fucked her through the evening and into the wee morning hours. They permitted her to doze on a couple of occasions, but soon awakened her. Sometimes they took her singly as the other watched and recouped, other times they each fucked her in quick succession—and once more they double-teamed her. Finally, as morning drew near, Jack carried her sated, limp form into their large walk-in shower.

He adjusted the dual showerheads to a warm spray, and he and Matt lathered their hands with her favorite bath gel and washed her. They supported her with their bodies, their gentle hands soaping her everywhere: her breasts, her underarms, the folds of her pussy, the crack of her ass, between her toes, her navel.

She sighed as their slick hands caressed her body. The cold, harsh light of day approached, and she wanted to cling to the fairytale, didn't want to face what would happen when she and Jack were alone.

She knew from experience, that even if it excited them, most men were unable to accept their girlfriends fucking other men. Had she destroyed her chance of happiness with Jack?

Morgan should have been exhausted of all desire, but they had sensitized her body to their touch and their soapy caresses rekindled her hunger. Jack's fingers delicately stroked her folds, and she whimpered as her clit pulsed to life.

"Sorry, Sweetheart. You're sore aren't you?"

She ached, yes, but she could be sore later. The magical evening wouldn't last forever. She shook her head and peered up at him. Her lips parted. She wasn't the only one aroused by the bathing. Jack was already at full staff and Matt's cock was starting to rise to the occasion.

Her arms snaked around Jack's neck. "One more time, okay?" Her fantasy evening was dissolving with the soap running off her deliciously achy body, and she wanted one last memory to carry next to her heart. Who knew what morning would bring? All she could count on was this moment, and she intended to savor every last ounce of gratification.

"Morgan...I don't want to hurt you. I don't think—" His cock pulsed against her abdomen.

"Don't think," she said. "Feel." She unwound herself and glided toward Matt, stopping when her nipples brushed his chest. She glanced over her shoulder at Jack. "Watch me, then do me. One more time."

Her tongue flicked Matt's pierced nipples before licking a trail to his cock. Morgan shifted, positioning herself so Jack could see her pleasuring his best friend. She wanted, hoped he'd be as turned on watching it as she was doing it. She laved Matt's smooth purple cock head, savoring him as if he were an all day sucker. Matt's fingers tangled in her slick, wet hair.

She planted her feet wide to present Jack with a view of her swollen sex and puckered asshole. The shower spray massaged her back, ran in an erotic steam over her crack, her cunt lips, her pulsing clit. She spread her legs wider, standing on tiptoes. The water teased and caressed her clit, her pussy, but it wasn't the water's touch she longed for.

"You're going to kill me, Morgan." Jack ground out, and though her mouth was full of cock, she smiled. She could hear the lust; he was on the verge of surrendering. Her stomach quickened in erotic anticipation.

"For God's sake, Jack. Give the lady what she wants and fuck her already," Matt growled. Rewarding him for his support, she drew him deep and sucked hard.

Jack touched her then, his fingers gently exploring her, teasing the rim of her asshole, dipping inside her cunt, stroking her swollen pussy lips, circling her clit. His passionate, loving touch filled her heart with joy. He caressed her until desire had her mewing like a feral kitten, then he placed his erection to her slit and sank into her. She clenched her muscles, moved against him, and he groaned, the rough sound resonating deep in her own chest. She felt wanted, needed, adored.

He loved her with his cock, caressing, stroking, suppressing his own needs, to pleasure her. The familiar, excruciatingly blissful burn ignited in her core and flashed outward. Her body shuddered, her cry of release strangled by Matt's cock as her climax rocked through her. Stars exploded behind her eyelids.

Jack hadn't come yet, but Matt was on the edge as Jack pulled out and sought the tight ring of her anus. After an evening of activity, her body easily and eagerly accepted his massive tool. He slid in deep, then pulled out, re-entering again and again, letting her close and open, experience him anew each time.

She purred in pleasure, and Jack's body succumbed, pumping in earnest. The ease with which their bodies now merged and the decadent rapture of the evening converged into one singular moment of passion. To shed all restraints, all inhibitions and follow the dictates of her heart, mind and soul represented the sweetest rapture of all.

She'd never been so connected to Jack, never experienced such utter fulfillment. Her hips matched Jack's thrusts, urging him to take his pleasure, wanting him to feel what she felt. She drew hard on Matt's cock, wanting to pleasure him as well. He shouted as he came in her mouth.

Jack groaned, spilled his seed, and Morgan felt complete.

**

She stood, bemused, as they patted her dry with a thick, thirsty, soft towel. Jack gently detangled her hair with a comb, then drew the towel tightly around her.

"Hold her," he said to Matt. "I want to change the sheets."

Matt settled her on his lap, sitting on the small padded bench at her vanity. His arms wrapped around her.

This friend of the man she loved had fucked her to screaming delight for hours, yet it felt odd to be held in his arms. Not unpleasant, but odd.

"You're one potent package, Morgan Moran," Matt said. "I always thought you were a hot chick, but I never realized how fiery you really are. Jack is a lucky son of a bitch."

"I, um, get the impression that you and Jack have done this before."

"We used to, but these days he's been flying solo. I was surprised when he asked if I wanted to join you. Pleased, but surprised." He paused. "Janine is going to be jealous."

Oh, God. Janine. Guilt slammed into her. How could she have forgotten Matt's girlfriend? Morgan was all for open and honest sex between consenting adults, but she abhorred cheating.

"Not for the reason you think," Matt amended quickly. "Janine, uh, plays for both teams. She's hot for you. I called her last night and told her where I was."

Morgan's jaw dropped. She remembered him making a call before joining her and Jack in the bedroom.

Matt laughed.

"Does that shock you?"

"No, not shock exactly. I just never suspected." Her mind reeled with the newest revelation. She must have fallen through some portal in a parallel but topsy-turvy world. Her sexually conservative Jack was really a raging bull who could fuck all night and had a history of threesomes. His best friend lusted after her, and so did the friend's bisexual girlfriend. And she had never guessed.

Morgan had always thought of Janine as an Amazon queen. Tall, with long straight blue-black hair, the muscled legs of a runner, and the largest breasts Morgan had ever seen outside of a porno flick. She put Morgan's modest 34Bs to shame.

"Janine has beautiful breasts," she said wistfully.

"Bodacious," he agreed. "But you also have great tits. Fresh, firm and sweet with succulent nipples."

She smiled. "Thank you."

Matt shifted her on his lap. "Have you ever had sex with another chick?"

"Once. A friend in college was exploring her sexuality. We finished a bottle of wine one night and…we played around a little." She shrugged. "It was pleasant, but I prefer men."

"What happened to your friend?"

"She fell in love with a great guy, married, had three kids and lives in Poughkeepsie."

"If you ever decide you want to try it again, I know Janine would love to walk you through it, so to speak."

What did she say to that? Thank you for the offer? "I'll pass, but if I change my mind, I'll let you know." She paused. "Have you and Jack and Janine ever…"

"A few times. But not since you two hooked up. Jack's a one-woman man. He hasn't been with anyone else since you came into the picture."

But she had—with Matt. Doubt gnawed at her. She desperately hoped her uninhibited behavior wouldn't change Jack's feelings. Her stomach flip-flopped as a new fear surfaced. What if his feelings already had changed? What if he had shared her because he no longer cared? What if she had lost him already? A heavy sadness swelled within her at the thought.

Jack pushed through the bathroom door. "I'm done."

He undid her towel and scooped her naked body off Matt's lap. Carrying her into the bedroom, he laid her on the mattress. The rumpled, sex and sweat-soaked sheets had been replaced by clean, crisp new ones that slid like heaven against her skin. Exhausted, she relaxed with a sigh, ignoring the blushing sky outside the window.

Matt donned his clothes then came over to the bed.

His crooked smile held a touch of self-satisfaction but also tenderness. "I'm off. My buddy Jack will take good care of you." He placed a light kiss on her mouth. "You knocked my socks off, Morgan. I hope we do this again sometime."

"Bye, Matt. You were great, too."

With a salute to Jack, Matt departed.

"Matt was right. You were fantastic. Fucking-A fantastic." Jack uncapped a bottle of oil heating in a warmer on the bed stand. He poured the oil into his palm and massaged the sweet-smelling liquid onto her body. "We need to talk, Morgan."

Her stomach fluttered. "I know…I uh…know."

"We don't need to do it now."

"Okay." Heart thumping with anxiety, she was only too willing to agree.

His fingers worked the soreness from her muscles, moisturized the chafed skin of her breasts, her inner thighs, her vulva. He massaged her backside, taking particular care with her tender bottom.

"Mmm." Under his soothing hands, her fears subsided. She needed to mull over what had happened, but she couldn't think straight, couldn't keep her heavy eyelids open. He was still massaging her when she fell asleep.

***

Her body was curved into Jack's hard-muscled form spoon-style, his hand cupping her breast, when Morgan awakened. She blinked against the glaring light streaming in through the billowing curtains. Her gaze darted to the bedside clock and widened as she saw it was nearly noon.

Careful to not disturb Jack's slumber, she stretched, stifling a groan as sore muscles protested. A tidal wave of memories, sensations, images, sounds, smells, thoughts, and emotions crashed over her.

Jack's hand tightened, and she craned her neck to find him awake.

"Good morning." he said, evenly.

"Good morning," she responded, wondering if it really

would be.

"How do you feel?" He peered at her.

Wonderfully Alive. Sexually sated. Deliciously sore. Scared.

She took a deep breath and exhaled. "Perfect." Liar.

"Good." His arms released her. "Happy birthday, by the way."

"Thank you. But it's not my birthday, anymore."

"It still is in my book." He bolted upright. "How about some cake? You never did have a piece."

Cake? After a year and a half of ho-hum sex, he and his buddy had taken turns fucking her, fulfilling every fantasy—and he wanted cake? What happened to "we need to talk?"

She regarded him, noticing his eager, half-nervous expression. She remembered the lopsidedness of the cake and her assessment that he'd baked it himself. Was he seeking approval of his baking? Was he worried she wouldn't like it?

Recalling how she botched his surprise party, she relented. "All right. That sounds good."

"I'll go get it." Naked, he bounded out of bed, and she noticed marks she'd left on him, love bites on his neck, his shoulders, his abdomen. He disappeared into the other room.

Morgan eased out of bed, wincing. She shuffled to the bathroom like a bowlegged cowboy who'd spent too much time in the saddle. She understood why her pussy, her asshole, and her jaw ached, but who knew sex used so many other muscles?

Morgan inspected herself in the mirror. Her chin, breasts, inner thighs and vulva were chafed from stubbled faces rasping against her skin. Her normally pink nipples were red and still erect from the attention they'd received. And very sore, she discovered as she touched one experimentally.

She pursed her lips, kissed swollen and rosy. Hollywood starlets would pay good money to have their lips surgically enhanced to look the way hers did now.

A love bite marred her nape where Matt had bitten her. She had two others, one on her inner thigh, another on her breast that she didn't remember receiving. She was surprised she didn't have more. Sucking, licking, nipping, teasing, tormenting, their mouths had been everywhere.

So had their hands and fingers. And their cocks. God, their cocks. Sensations rewound through her mind. The fullness, the tension, the pressure. The shattering orgasms. Real life rarely compared to one's fantasies; last night it had exceeded them.

Despite the thorough fucking and the resultant soreness, her pussy responded to the memory, growing moist.

Jack's desire had been insatiable. She'd never experienced him like that, and she clung to the hope that it was good, that it meant something more than sex, that she still meant something to him. Throughout the evening, he'd encouraged her uninhibited, abandoned response with heated glances and hoarse words of approval. He'd enjoyed her body, and seemed to draw pleasure from her enjoyment.

But what did that mean, really?

How did Jack feel now? Was she just a playmate, a good-time girl? Or was she the person he wanted to spend his life with? Did he still love her? Did he ever really love her?

He'd cuddled and stroked her after each sexual round, gently washed her body, massaged her aches, and held her as she slept. He'd been tender as well as passionate, and she drew hope from that.

But when she boiled it all down, she had no real, concrete idea what Jack wanted—other than cake.

She finished her business in the bathroom and returned to the bedroom.

Morgan had just settled on the bed, tucked the covers under her armpits, when Jack returned with one square of cake, the corner with the heart.

"I put some coffee on." He handed her the plate and a fork.

She looked at him. "You're not having any?"

"I had some yesterday."

"Oh."

His eyes riveted on her, and he perched on the bed, waiting

for her to try it. Once again, she got the impression he was nervous.

"I'm sure it's very good." She smiled and forked a small bit. She watched him watch her as she lifted it to her mouth.

It was strawberry with cream cheese icing. And good, she discovered. "It's wonderful. Did you bake this?" Her stomach rumbled, reminding her she hadn't eaten since lunchtime the day before. She took another bite.

"Yes." He continued to regard her steadily, and she wondered if he was going to wait until she finished the entire piece.

Feeling awkward, she forked another piece and hit a hard lump, something metal. She poked the object with her fork. What should she do now? Tell him? Pretend there was nothing there?

"Something wrong with the cake?" His gaze was intent.

"There, uh, seems to be something in it."

She used her fork to scoop up the object. Hooked on the tines was a ring. A band. With a stone. A large, sparkling stone. She started to tremble. "Oh, my God!" Morgan's gaze flew from the ring to Jack's face. Her heart clenched painfully.

Jack took the sticky, cake-coated ring from her, and grasping her trembling left hand, slipped it on her finger. "Morgan Moran, I love you so much. Will you marry me? Will you be my lover, my best friend…my wife?

She burst into tears. "I was afraid you didn't love m-me anymore. After last night, I thought you didn't w-want me. Or only wanted to fuck me. That I wasn't good enough for you anymore."

"Not love you? Not want you? Oh, Morgan." Jack grabbed her in a hug. The cake tumbled from her grasp. Her sticky hand was pressed against his thumping heart.

"You're the best thing that ever happened to me. I love you so much. I always will." He kissed the tears streaming from her eyes. "Last night only made me want you more. I love that you're so uninhibited, so open to sexual pleasure."

She sniffed. "Matt told me you haven't been with anyone

else since we've been together."

He nodded. "That's true. You're all the woman I want."

"But now I have!'

"That's not the same." He shook his head. "The threesome with Matt was an experience I wanted to give you. Don't you know it thrills me to see you take your pleasure that way?"

His voice dropped to a throaty, mesmerizing rumble. "You enjoyed it, didn't you, having your pussy licked and your nipples sucked simultaneously... ...sucking cock as you were being fucked...having your tight pussy and your even tighter ass filled at the same time?"

Her pussy released a gush of wetness. "Yes," she admitted in a whisper. "It was thrilling, wild, magical. Better than I could ever have imagined."

"I want that for you." His thumb traced her lower lip.

"But why now? Matt said you used to do ménages. But until last night, you never indicated you wanted a threesome. Or that you liked anal sex. Our sex life was always so "

"Boring?"

"Vanilla." She corrected. "Why didn't you tell me you wanted variety?"

"Why didn't you tell me?"

"I was afraid I'd shock you."

"Same for me." He sighed. "Many women don't go for it. I was engaged once. She dumped me after I suggested things she considered 'perverted.' I was afraid I'd scare you away if I told you what I wanted."

He paused. "It wasn't until I spanked you, and you creamed all over my pants, that I thought I had a chance."

She looked down at the ring. "But you bought this before that, right?"

"I love you Morgan. You're the only woman for me. Whether we have vanilla sex—which I still like, by the way—or pecan-peppermint-pistachio swirl."

"Oh, Jack." She twined her arms around his neck, pressing her bare breasts to his chest, squishing the cake between them.

"I love you, too. So much. I'd be proud to be your wife."

"I'd be proud to be your husband," he said and bore her down on the bed. He licked her nipple, covered by smashed cake and cream cheese icing. He lifted his head and grinned. "You know, vanilla sex goes real good with birthday cake."

She smeared frosting on the length his erect cock. "So it does."

She smiled.

It was possible to have her cake and eat it, too.

THE END

Visit The Black Velvet Seductions Blog

http://www.blackvelvetseductions.com/readers_blog/

Prizes! Prizes! Prizes!
Frequent Kindle Giveaways
Amazon Gift Cards
Paperbacks
Ebooks
Lace Bookmarks
Book Bags
Too Many Other Prizes To List

Winners announced each Saturday at
http://www.blackvelvetseductions.com/readers_blog/

Available Now From Black Velvet Seductions

Other books by
Richard Savage

The Crimson Z

Temporally Yours & The Key

Available Now in
Paperback and ebook
www.blackvelvetseductions.com

Available Now From Black Velvet Seductions

Other books by
Starla Kaye

Holly's Big Bad Santa

Her Cowboy's Way
Domestic Discipline Anthology

Available Now in
Paperback and ebook
www.blackvelvetseductions.com

Lightning Source UK Ltd.
Milton Keynes UK
22 October 2010

161718UK00001B/16/P